"Will you help me?" she pleaded

Paige's voice broke then. "They told me they'd kill her. They're keeping her in the dark. Katie hates the dark."

"How do you think I can help? I don't know you and I sure don't know them. What do you want me to do, offer myself to them?" Jay asked.

She met his gaze. "The Johnny I knew would have done anything in his power to protect a child."

Jay's heart slammed into his chest with the force of a blow. *The Johnny she'd known.* "And you think I'm that man?" he asked, the effort of holding hope at bay inside him too much.

She held his gaze for a moment, her eyes wide and haunted. If he wasn't careful, she could make him believe it himself....

Dear Harlequin Intrigue Reader,

Happy Valentine's Day! We are so pleased you've come back to Harlequin Intrigue for another exciting month of breathtaking romantic suspense.

And our February lineup is sure to please, starting with another installment in Debra Webb's trilogy about the most covert agents around: THE SPECIALISTS. *Her Hidden Truth* is a truly innovative story about what could happen if an undercover agent had a little help from a memory device to ensure her cover. But what if said implant malfunctioned and past, present and future were all mixed up? Fortunately this lucky lady has a very sexy recovery Specialist to extract her from the clutches of a group of dangerous terrorists.

Next we have another title in our TOP SECRET BABIES promotion by Mallory Kane, called *Heir to Secret Memories*. Though a bachelor heir to a family fortune is stricken with amnesia, he can't forget one very beautiful woman. And when she comes to him in desperation to locate her child, he's doubly astonished to find out he is the missing girl's father.

Julie Miller returns to her ongoing series THE TAYLOR CLAN with *The Rookie*. If you go for those younger guys, well, hold on to your hats, because Josh Taylor is one dynamite lawman.

Finally, Amanda Stevens takes up the holiday baton with *Confessions of the Heart*. In this unique story, a woman receives a heart transplant and is inexorably drawn to the original owner's husband. Find out why in this exceptional story.

Enjoy all four!

Sincerely,

Denise O'Sullivan
Associate Senior Editor
Harlequin Intrigue

HEIR TO SECRET MEMORIES

MALLORY KANE

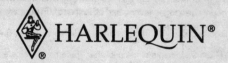

TORONTO • NEW YORK • LONDON
AMSTERDAM • PARIS • SYDNEY • HAMBURG
STOCKHOLM • ATHENS • TOKYO • MILAN • MADRID
PRAGUE • WARSAW • BUDAPEST • AUCKLAND

ISBN 0-373-22698-5

HEIR TO SECRET MEMORIES

Copyright © 2003 by Rickey R. Mallory

This edition published by arrangement with Harlequin Books S.A.

® and TM are trademarks of the publisher. Trademarks indicated with
® are registered in the United States Patent and Trademark Office, the
Canadian Trade Marks Office and in other countries.

Visit us at www.eHarlequin.com

Printed in U.S.A.

ABOUT THE AUTHOR

Mallory Kane took early retirement from her position as assistant chief of pharmacy at a large metropolitan medical center to pursue her other loves: writing and art. She has published and won awards for science fiction and fantasy, as well as romance. Mallory credits her love of books to her mother, who taught her that books are a precious resource and should be treated with loving respect. Her grandfather and her father were both steeped in the Southern tradition of oral history, and could hold an audience spellbound with their storytelling skills. Mallory aspires to be as good a storyteller as her father. She loves romantic suspense with dangerous heroes and dauntless heroines. She is also fascinated by story ideas that explore the infinite capacity of the brain to adapt and develop higher skills.

Mallory lives in Mississippi with her husband and their dauntless cat. She would be delighted to hear from readers. You can write to her c/o Harlequin Books, 300 East 42nd Street, Sixth Floor, New York, NY 10017.

Books by Mallory Kane

HARLEQUIN INTRIGUE
620—THE LAWMAN WHO LOVED HER
698—HEIR TO SECRET MEMORIES

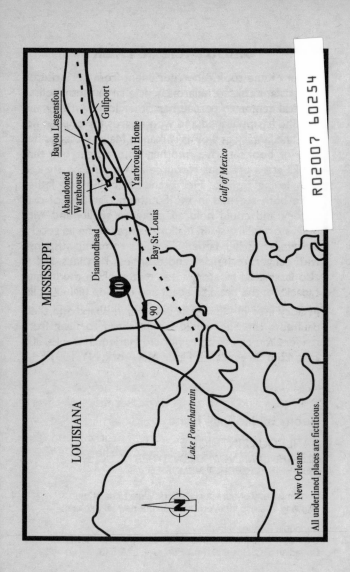

MISSISSIPPI

Bayou Lesgensfou

Gulfport

Abandoned
Warehouse

Yarbrough Home

Diamondhead

Bay St. Louis

10

90

Gulf of Mexico

LOUISIANA

Lake Pontchartrain

New Orleans

N

All underlined places are fictitious.

CAST OF CHARACTERS

Paige Reynolds—When her daughter is kidnapped, she must enlist the help of the lover who deserted her years ago, or her daughter will die.

Johnny Yarbrough—Heir to the Yarbrough fortune, he was kidnapped and presumed dead three years ago.

Jay Wellcome—Three years ago he woke with a bullet wound and no memories. Now a woman he recognizes only from nightmarish visions is asking him to help her find a child she says is his.

Katie Yarbrough—Seven years old, she's the image of her mother, with her father's dark blue eyes. She's a courageous little girl, if she can just hold on until her mom can find her.

Serena Yarbrough—She married Johnny's father for money, and her scheme to control the Yarbrough fortune worked. But now her past is catching up with her. Can she succeed in eliminating the rightful heirs this time?

Leonard Lynch—Serena's brother. If he's clever enough to find Paige and Johnny, they may never live to rescue their child.

Sally McGowan—Paige's entrepreneurial friend. She invited Serena to her art exhibit, but she would never harm Katie, would she?

For Joyce, who kept me sane.

Prologue

Summer, seven years ago

Paige Reynolds woke up the way she had since the day her mother died, scared, lonely, praying it was all a dream and her mom was in their tiny kitchen, making coffee. But a deep breath yielded no delicious aroma of coffee, just an ache of grief in her heart.

Then through the haze of sleep she heard the comforting scratch of pencil against paper.

Johnny.

She was safe and warm and loved. Johnny was here and he was doing what he did so often. Drawing her while she slept.

She opened her eyes to meet his sapphire-blue gaze.

"Morning, Tiger," he said softly.

He had on faded jeans and no shirt. His brown hair was tousled and that cowlick stuck up in the back.

Her heart filled to bursting with love. She'd never been as happy in the entire seventeen years of her life as during these past six weeks.

"You're up early." She didn't want to get up yet. They'd spent most of the night making love.

Johnny had been quiet, more intense than usual. He'd held her and loved her and pressed kisses along every inch of her as if she were some precious icon and he were an obsessed worshiper. He'd acted as though he were memorizing her, body and soul, so he'd never forget her.

His fierce passion had been a little scary. But he'd whispered "I love you" a thousand times, and finally, as dawn reddened the sky, she'd fallen asleep feeling safe and sheltered in his warm, strong arms.

Just thinking about the night made her body thrill. She sat up in bed, letting the sheet fall behind her. Looking over her shoulder at him, she smiled. "You sure you're ready to get up?"

He made a low, growling sound in his throat, threw the sketchpad aside and dove into bed with her.

Afterward, she lay in the crook of his arm while his fingers brushed lightly through her hair.

"Paige?"

"Hmm?"

"Have you thought about what you're going to do?"

Her hazy glow faded a bit. "What do you mean?"

He kissed her cheek. "It's been over three months since your mother died. What are you planning? Can you afford to go back to school in September?"

His question sent her heart hammering against her chest. Claws of panic began to tear at her insides, just like they had each week since her mother had succumbed to ovarian cancer as she counted her waitressing tips, praying there was enough money to pay the rent one more time. She sat up, pulling the sheet protectively against her.

"I thought we..." she started, but as soon as she

said the words, as soon as she brought her gaze up to meet his, she knew.

"You're leaving." Her voice cracked on the last word.

"Paige, no. Wait." Johnny sat up too, and grabbed her arms. "Listen to me."

But she was already withdrawing into her protective shell. It had always just been her and her mother. Then when her mother died, her whole focus had been on survival.

But that was before Johnny had seen her in Jackson Square and asked if he could sketch her. Before he'd brought love and sunshine back into her life.

She'd believed Johnny's words of love, just like her mother had believed her father. But when her mother had gotten pregnant, her father had revealed that he already had a wife and family. He had abandoned her mother when she needed him most. And now Johnny was leaving her.

Her breath caught in a sob.

"Paige!" He shook her, gently but firmly. "I love you. Weren't you listening last night? I love you. Wait a minute." He jumped up, his naked body pale and beautifully lit by the sunlight shining through the apartment windows. He got something from his backpack and came back to the bed.

"Give me your left hand."

Hesitantly, Paige held out her hand, which shook. *Don't leave me,* her heart screamed. *I love you.*

She watched his face as he took her hand in his.

"God, you're shaking," he whispered. "I didn't mean to scare you. I did it all wrong."

She felt something cool slip onto her finger.

"What…"

Johnny pulled her hand to his chest and placed his hand over it. She felt his heart beating fast, felt the warm familiar comfort of his hand over hers. "This was my mother's ring. Father had it made especially for her. She wore it till the day she died. I want you to wear it."

He looked at her solemnly. "I love you. I will love you forever. Will you marry me?"

A sharp pain pierced her breast. "M-marry?"

He nodded, and a lock of hair fell over his forehead. "I have to go back to school too, now that summer's over. Come with me to Boston. We can live together. Be married. You could go to school up there."

"M-married?"

Johnny laughed and kissed her. "M-m-m-married. Now stop stuttering and say yes."

Paige's eyes burned with tears. When her mother had died, she'd been left to face a world she wasn't prepared for. In the weeks that followed, she had learned the meaning of the word alone.

"Oh, Johnny. I thought you were leaving me."

A shadow crossed Johnny's face. "I'm never going to leave you. I love you. I just have to take care of one thing. My father's not going to be very happy about this." His mouth twisted. "He's never happy about anything I do these days."

He jumped up and pulled on his jeans. "So I just need to run home and talk to him. I want him to meet you. He'll love you once he meets you."

Paige felt as if she were on a merry-go-round that had gone out of control. Her head was spinning. She put her hand over her fluttering heart.

He wanted to marry her. Marry! She was seventeen

and all alone in the world. He was probably twenty and…. She suddenly realized she didn't know much about him, except that he wanted to be an artist, but his father disapproved.

But he loved her. He wanted to marry her.

"How long have you been thinking about this?" she asked, grabbing one of his white monogrammed shirts and pulling it on, pushing the long sleeves back so she could fasten the buttons.

Johnny was gathering up stuff and throwing it in his backpack. He shrugged. "From the first time I saw you in Jackson Square. You were the most beautiful thing I'd ever seen. I knew I had to draw that classic face."

He turned and threw his arms wide. "Then you smiled and stole my heart."

She giggled. "I didn't know you were in school. Where'd you say?"

Johnny shot her a sharp glance. "Harvard."

Paige flopped down on the bed. *Harvard?* They'd been together six weeks and she'd never known he went to Harvard. A tiny hummingbird of fear began to flutter in her breast. "Harvard? Are you rich or something?"

He shook his head as he slid his sketchpad into a pocket of his backpack. "Something," he muttered.

He was avoiding her eyes. She wanted to stop him, make him look at her. She wanted him to promise her everything was going to be perfect. That he would love her forever and never leave her.

After spending a few seconds adjusting the zippers on his pack, he came over and cupped her face in his two hands.

"Come on, Tiger, don't look so scared. We're go-

ing to have a wonderful life, I promise." He kissed
her, then murmured something and pulled her tightly
to him and deepened the kiss, his warm body hard
against her. Her body molded to his and her insides
grew liquid with yearning.

Oh, she loved him.

Moaning in frustration, he pulled away reluctantly.
"I've got to get out of here."

Paige bit her lip and tried to think clearly. He was
leaving, and that scared her, but then he was coming
back. "Where does your father live?"

"Up the Mississippi Coast," he said as he set his
backpack near the door. "Not far."

Paige still felt like that merry-go-round was out of
control. "Johnny, stop for a minute and talk to me.
How will you get there?"

"My car."

"You have a car?"

He turned around, smiling wryly. "Sure. A Mustang Cobra. Now listen. I'll spend the night at home,
and then by tomorrow I'll have the old man convinced. He'll be dying to meet you. So wait for me
here."

That hummingbird's wings sped up in her breast,
stirring up the memories of her mother alone in her
room, night after night, crying over a man who had
never loved her. She tried to ignore them, rubbing her
thumb over the ring as if it could create magic. As if
it would bring him back to her.

"Maybe I should go with you now," she suggested.

His face shut down and he pushed his fingers
through his hair. "It wouldn't be a good idea. Like I
said, my father will take some convincing. And trust

me, you don't want to hear what my stepmother will
have to say. I'll be back here no later than three
o'clock tomorrow afternoon. I promise.''

Then he grinned and grabbed her, hugging her
tight, and bent his head to give her another mind-
drugging kiss.

"I love you, Paige Reynolds. Soon to be Mrs. Yarbrough.''

Paige smiled a little shakily. "I love you, too. More
than you can imagine. Don't be late. I'll wait for you,
right here.''

"You'd better.'' He took her left hand and kissed
her palm, then turned it over and kissed the ring.

"And don't take off this ring. Not for anything. It's
magic.'' He grinned and his blue eyes sparkled. "It'll
bring me back to you.''

He picked up his pack and left, closing her apartment door behind him.

Paige stared at the door for a moment, bringing the
ring up to her lips as he had.

Magic. He'd said what she'd been thinking. It must
be true.

She ran to the window.

Down on Urselines Street, he slung his pack over
his shoulder and looked up. He waved, then walked
away toward the levee, his loose-limbed, graceful
stride as familiar to her as his face.

Paige watched until he disappeared around the corner. As soon as he was out of sight, panic grabbed at
her heart again. She pushed it away.

"I'm going to be married,'' she whispered in awe,
sitting down on the bed. "Married.'' She flung her
arms wide and flopped down on her back.

"Mrs. John Yarbrough.'' Her thumb caressed the
ring. Her life was never going to be the same again.

Chapter One

Today

Edging a bit closer to the front door of Sally Mc-Gowan's chic Garden District home, Paige smiled sadly at the irony. Seven years ago she'd been an orphaned, pregnant teenager, scared and alone, forced to accept the grudging, disapproving charity of her aunt.

Now she was a well-respected social worker. The road had been hard, the hours of studying and working and taking care of her daughter brutal, but she had done what her mother had never been able to do. She'd put her heartbreak behind her and concentrated all her love and energy on her career and on Kate, her beloved child.

Tonight she found herself in a roomful of over-dressed, snobbish people who were here to pay inflated prices for mediocre art to raise money for other sad young girls. And by the same token, make themselves feel generous and altruistic.

Paige took another step and smiled at a young man who was watching her curiously. Several people had looked at her that way this evening. She touched her cheek. Was there something wrong with her hair or makeup?

Someone bumped into her. It was a short, plump man dressed in white tie and tails with an honest to goodness monocle that popped off his eye and dangled by its silver chain.

''Excuse me,'' she said automatically, biting her lip to keep from laughing. He looked just like a penguin. He harumphed and waddled away.

Was it just her or did everyone here tonight look like cartoon characters? Earlier she'd seen a sour-faced woman with a white streak in her coal-black hair and a white wrap with what looked suspiciously like Dalmatian spots on it.

Chuckling to herself, Paige wished her daughter, Katie, was here. Paige had never been good at being pompous and chic, and she and Katie could have a blast matching these folks with their cartoon counterparts.

She looked at her watch. Katie had been indignant when Sally had sprung the last-minute invitation on Paige. Tonight was supposed to be pizza night, plus tomorrow Katie started her second year of swimming lessons.

Paige had promised herself she'd be home by eleven, and it was already eleven-thirty.

Tossing her long blond braid over her shoulder, she threaded her way through the crowd to tell Sally she was leaving, and practically collided with the woman in the Dalmatian-spotted wrap.

Paige hastily apologized. But the woman not only looked like the cartoon villainess, she behaved like her, too. She waved away Paige's apology as if she were shooing a fly and sucked on the cigarette dangling from her long, shiny holder.

The woman's hostile gaze swept disdainfully over Paige's black skirt and silver blouse before she turned her back.

Something about her seemed vaguely familiar—not many women had such a prominent streak in their hair. Maybe Paige had seen her at another charity event.

Just then Sally sailed into the room, her flowing red gown with sleeves that draped to the floor drawing every eye.

"Well?" Stopping in front of Paige, Sally gestured theatrically, sloshing champagne from a crystal flute. "Did you see it?"

"See what?" Paige asked.

"My latest discovery. Haven't you wondered why people keep staring at you? Remember, I promised you an evening you wouldn't soon forget."

A tinge of unease tightened Paige's belly as her friend ushered her toward the east wall of the room. Sally's surprises were predictably obscure. "I saw the ice sculpture," she ventured.

"Not the ice sculpture." Sally waved her arm. "My newest artist."

Everything Sally did was dramatic, from her famous charity soirees to the way she scoured the city dressed in her talent-hunting uniform of designer jeans and a shapeless, ancient men's suit jacket that would do a homeless man proud, topped by an equally disreputable fedora.

Paige smiled indulgently. "Have you been prowling through dusty junk shops again?"

"Of course. It's the best way in the world to discover new artists. I found this one in a musty little voodoo shop down near the docks. It's the surprise I promised you.''

A framed drawing hung by itself in the center of an alcove. As Sally stepped aside, the crowd of people seemed to melt back into the paneling.

Paige stiffened as her vision telescoped in on the picture.

''Oh my God,'' she choked, shock stealing her breath and tightening like a vise around her throat.

It was a small piece, sketched in charcoal. There wasn't much to it, just a few perfectly executed lines. Only the eyes were fully drawn, but Paige recognized herself, much younger, looking over her naked shoulder with mischief in her glance.

''Voilà!'' She heard Sally's throaty laugh. She felt all eyes on her.

''Isn't it stunning? And the resemblance is phenomenal.''

Sally's voice echoed in her head like music from the next room, heard but not recognized. Her thoughts were on another time. She remembered the very day. It was the day Johnny had asked her to marry him, the day he'd given her his mother's ring and promised her he would love her forever.

The last time she'd ever seen him.

Paige squeezed her eyes shut and clenched her teeth. It couldn't be Johnny. That was another life. Johnny was dead.

Consciously relaxing her arms, she forced herself to smile. ''It's not me,'' she said tightly. ''It's just one of those amazing coincidences.''

She stepped close to Sally, whose smile was fading

a bit. "Where did you get that? You should have warned me," she whispered.

"I bought it for you. I just wanted to display it first. Do you know the artist?"

Paige shook her head and started to turn away, but Sally pointed and her long red fingernail drew Paige's eye back toward the sketch.

As sudden as a punch in the stomach, Paige's diaphragm seized as she focused on the signature. Three letters in a unique stylized script, followed by an anchor in the shape of a Y. It was a design Paige would never forget, one she'd have sworn was embossed on her heart.

A shirt with that monogram on it was stuffed in a box, along with other mementos of a past that seemed like a long-forgotten dream.

For an instant, she ached to touch the letters, trace them with her fingers like she'd done long ago when she'd still believed in dreams. Her hand lifted, her fingers reached and she had to struggle to stop them from caressing the glass over the signature.

It couldn't be. The dead didn't come back to life.

Paige clenched her fist and forced her hand back down to her side.

"Paige Reynolds! You're not going to faint on me, are you? You're white as a sheet!"

Paige shook her head. "Where did you say you found it?" she asked, trying to lighten her voice.

Sally beamed, her face reflecting triumph. "One of those little streets down by the docks. Isn't the resemblance phenomenal? It's almost as if you sat for the artist."

Paige frowned. Sally's words sliced into her already aching heart. "Well, that's impossible," she replied flatly.

Then, aware of the attention they were receiving from the crowd, she pasted a false smile on her face.

"Thank you so much," she said through numb lips. "The drawing is beautiful. I must apologize, but I have to go. Katie's with a new sitter. I don't want to be late."

"A new sitter? I can see why you'd be concerned. Well, you must bring her for a visit soon. Maybe I should have a showing of children's art," Sally said. "Katie's six years old now, isn't she? She's such a little doll, with those beautiful dark-blue eyes of hers."

Paige's face felt stiff. "She was just six in May. I really have to go. I'll talk to you later this week."

"Call me tomorrow. We'll have lunch and you can pick up your drawing," Sally called as a handsome, elegant man touched her arm. She turned with a flourish, back in perfect hostess mode.

Paige's hands trembled, her throat hurt and her eyes burned. If she didn't know better, she might think she was about to cry, but Paige Reynolds never cried. Ever.

As she worked her way toward the door, fielding questions and comments about her resemblance to the drawing, she glanced back at it. The cartoon villainess stood nearby, eyes narrowed against the smoke curling up from her cigarette, watching her.

SERENA YARBROUGH LET cigarette smoke drift out through her nostrils. She'd overheard the little blonde's conversation with Sally McGowan. She dug her nails into her palms, barely restraining herself from tearing after the woman Sally had called Paige Reynolds.

She turned back to the drawing, adopting a bored expression as she scrutinized the signature that consisted of the letters JAY plus the old Yarbrough shipping logo.

That anchor had been the trademark logo of Yarbrough Shipping until two years ago when Serena had acquired several small and diverse companies, which transformed Yarbrough Shipping into Yarbrough Industries. She'd had the logo redesigned and updated.

Lifting the champagne flute, she managed not to bite into the glass as she sipped delicately. Aware that someone might be watching her, she forced her anger into a cold knot of resolve.

The signature on the drawing was unmistakable, but it was the date that made her want to rip her clothes and scream in anger and frustration.

This year.

Johnny Yarbrough was alive! Her stepson, the true heir to the Yarbrough fortune, had somehow managed to survive her scheme to get rid of him.

Her brother, Leonard, had assured her Johnny was dead when his goons had dumped his body into the river. She'd been outraged at the time. Now she had to force herself to remain calm as fury swirled in her breast.

She couldn't believe the fool hadn't known that the body might never be found if it drifted out into the Gulf.

As she'd feared, the body had never turned up. Only the stolen car with Johnny's bloodstained wallet in the trunk. At least the kidnappers had left no traceable evidence in the car.

After a court order had declared Johnny legally dead, based on the DNA evidence of his blood in the car, Serena's son Brandon—Madison Yarbrough's second son—was the sole heir, and Serena controlled the entire Yarbrough fortune.

But now, in the space of an evening her plans were ruined. The evidence that Johnny was still alive was displayed right before her eyes. Almost as if he were taunting her.

Then there was the woman who was obviously the model for the drawing. Sally was right; the resemblance was too close to be coincidence, no matter how much Paige Reynolds denied it. And Serena hadn't missed the way the woman's face drained of color when she saw it.

And if all that weren't enough, she was flaunting Johnny's mother's ring. It was a cheap little ring, but unmistakable, with sapphires in the shape of the old anchor logo. Madison had given it to his first wife, then to his son after she died.

One by one, Serena considered all the facts, like pieces of a puzzle and they all fitted into place.

Johnny was alive. And, judging by the conversation she'd overheard between Paige Reynolds and Sally, he had a daughter.

Six years old in May, the little blonde had said. That would put the child's conception at about the time of Johnny's rebellious summer bumming around the French Quarter, right after Serena had married his father.

Serena drew on her cigarette. That would make Johnny's child older than her son. Another heir to dilute the fortune that was rightfully hers. She still hated Madison for refusing to change his will, which named Johnny or his progeny as primary heir to the Yarbrough fortune. But she'd gotten rid of the barriers to Madison Yarbrough's fortune once, and she could do it again.

She'd taken care of that little problem and now she was in control. She planned to stay in control.

She watched as the young woman worked her way through the crowd toward the door. She nodded in satisfaction.

It was annoying that her stepson had cheated death. But now that Serena knew...

Draining her champagne glass and dropping the half-smoked cigarette into it, Serena pulled her cell phone out of her purse and dialed a number.

"I have an urgent job for you," she said quietly, stepping out onto the balcony for privacy. "Well, get *out* of bed and get down to the office. I have a test case for the new tracking technology."

As soon as she finished her call, she went looking for Sally. She needed every scrap of information Sally possessed on the artist and on Paige Reynolds.

The promise little Sue Ann Lynch had made to herself the day she ran away from the shabby trailer park and changed her name still festered inside her.

She would never be poor again.

The money was hers. Right now three people stood in her way: Johnny, his child, and the child's mother.

They all had to die.

DURING THE CAB RIDE HOME, Paige stared out the car window as the dark, colorful streets of New Orleans streaked by. A familiar ache started in the back of her throat, building until it felt like a pair of hands choking her.

It had been seven years since Johnny had walked out of her apartment and her life, over three years since he'd been declared dead, and still she missed him.

She pulled her long braid over her shoulder and played with the ends, her unseeing gaze on the streets outside.

When she'd seen the sketch, for an instant she'd been plunged back into the past, to the time when she still believed Johnny loved her and would come back for her. When she'd been sure she would never end up alone and pregnant like her mother.

The day she'd found out she was pregnant she'd vowed she would keep her daughter, no matter what she had to do.

She knew the pain of abandonment—the hollow, terrifying fear of having no one. Katie would never spend one day frightened and alone, not if Paige were alive to prevent it. She would give her life to keep her daughter safe.

Paige shook her head and tried to concentrate on the awful music from the cabbie's radio, but her brain wouldn't let go of the past. She recalled the day six years before when she'd happened to glance at the society page, the day she'd found out who Johnny really was.

He was the son of shipping magnate, Madison Yarbrough, heir to a fortune so vast she couldn't even imagine it. His family was *the* Yarbroughs.

Staring at a photograph of Johnny and his father captioned ''Son Follows In Father's Footsteps,'' Paige had finally seen her worst nightmare come true.

He had never cared about her or intended to marry her. Their whole relationship had been a lie. He'd just been a rich kid slumming. She'd imagined all sorts of horrible reasons he hadn't come back for her, but she'd never even considered the simplest one.

He hadn't wanted to.

Then three years later, she'd seen his photograph in the paper again. This time it was the sensational story of his kidnapping played out on TV. She'd waited with the rest of the city, suffered along with his father, until the police found the bloodstained car and concluded that John Andrew Yarbrough was dead.

Now her daughter was six years old, and Paige had struggled and sacrificed to create a good life for the two of them. A safe, steady life.

No odd coincidence of a drawing with a familiar signature could change that. There had to be another explanation.

Maybe someone had unearthed one of Johnny's old sketches and either unconsciously or deliberately copied the style and the signature. That would explain the recent date.

As bizarre as that idea was, it was easier for Paige to believe than the alternative...that Johnny wasn't dead at all. That he was alive and well, living his privileged life and selling sketches of their intimate moments as a lark.

She stirred as the cab stopped in front of her apartment.

As she paid the driver, a car door opened at the curb and a small figure dressed in very long jeans and a very short top got out. It was Katie's baby-sitter.

The teenager's painted eyes were wide under her short straight hair. "Ms. Reynolds, I was just—"

Concern about Katie sharpened Paige's voice.

"Dawn? What's going on here?" She looked toward her apartment. The front door was ajar.

Dawn pouted. "I was just…saying good-night to my boyfriend."

Paige grabbed the girl's arm. "Where is Katie?"

Dawn looked at her with eyes wide. "She's right inside. She's asleep."

Paige tightened her grip on the girl's arm. "You never, ever leave a child alone. Don't you know that? Not for an instant." She was so angry and worried that her voice shook.

"Katie's asleep, Ms. Reynolds," Dawn said in a small voice. "She's fine. I was only out here for a minute."

Rooting in her purse Paige found some bills. "Here. Have your boyfriend take you home."

As she ran toward the door, she called back to the girl. "I *will* be talking to your mother, Dawn."

Telling herself she was overreacting, but unable to shake her unease, Paige pushed the door open.

The first thing she saw was the phone lying in the middle of the living room floor, its torn cord twisted and raw, like the innards of a dead snake. She stared at it for a second, her brain not processing what she was seeing.

Katie!

She ran through the tiny hallway to Katie's room. "Katie?" she whispered.

No answer.

Paige pushed the door open. Dawn had assured her that Katie was sleeping, but something was wrong. The room felt odd—empty. She fumbled for the bed-side lamp with a trembling hand.

"Katie, sweetie. I'm home."

Light flooded the room. It looked just like it had earlier in the evening, except that the bedclothes were rumpled and her daughter was gone.

"It's okay. It's been a weird evening," she whispered, trying to calm her growing panic. Katie often slept in Paige's room.

"Katie!"

She ran into her bedroom, throwing on every light switch she passed, but Katie wasn't there.

"Katie." Her voice cracked. "Where are you?"

She put her hand over her mouth, trying to hold in a scream.

It's okay. It's probably nothing. But her heart knew her brain was lying.

The bedroom phone had been ripped from the wall, too. She stared at it. It lay on the floor, ominous proof of a truth so awful, Paige couldn't let herself believe it.

Her breath stuck in her throat.

She backed out of her bedroom and rushed into the little kitchen. The back door was open.

"Oh, no," she whispered. "Oh, no."

"Katie!" Tears streaked down her face and tasted like blood in her mouth. Somehow her shaky legs carried her back to Katie's bedroom.

She stared at the bed. It was so awfully empty, a small hollow in the pillow the only sign her daughter had been there.

She couldn't keep trying to fool herself. She knew. Her daughter was gone.

She touched the pillow, plumping it. She reached for the sheet, but her fingers couldn't hold on to the material.

"Oh, Katie." She put her hands over her mouth.

"Katie! Where are you?" she screamed into her hands.

Her gaze searched the room as if she might find her daughter hiding behind a chair, or under the bed. As if the last few minutes were just a bad dream and Katie was playing a joke.

There was a noise from somewhere in the room. It took a few seconds for the sound to penetrate Paige's anguish. She lifted her head. What was it?

The noise sounded again, a terrible, electronically cheerful chirp in the middle of Paige's horror.

"A cell phone?" she muttered. Was that a cell phone? She didn't have a cell phone. It was here, somewhere, in Katie's room.

She rooted through the bedclothes, tossing pillows, pulling off the bedspread.

There it was, lying like a big black bug in her daughter's bed. She grabbed it, jabbing at buttons that seemed stuck or broken. Finally one gave.

"Hello? Hello? Who is this?" she screamed, terror paralyzing her, darkening her vision.

She listened, but there was no sound.

"Please...who is this? Katie?" she cried.

Still nothing but silence.

"Talk to me!" she shouted, then shook the phone, desperation giving way to frustration. "Answer me! Where is my daughter?"

"Now, now, Paige, there's no need to shout. Your daughter is just fine," an obviously disguised voice said.

She almost dropped the phone. Relief burned through her like a firestorm. Her throat closed. "Who is this? Where is Katie?" she croaked.

"I told you, she's fine." The raspy whisper—Paige

couldn't tell if it were male or female—sounded impatient.

"Let me talk to her."

"All in good time."

"I have to talk to her!" She gripped the phone in both hands, hunched over it as if she could somehow get closer to Katie by doing so.

"All you have to do is listen."

"But—"

"No! You will be allowed to talk to Katie when you obey. When you don't obey…"

Paige's heart turned to ice. Whoever was on the other end of the phone had kidnapped her daughter. They were threatening to hurt her. The flat, emotionless voice promised horrible, unthinkable things.

"O-okay," she stammered. "I'll do whatever you want. Please don't hurt her. Please!"

"Now listen carefully. I will only say this once. Bring me Johnny Yarbrough."

"What?" Paige's hand tightened reflexively on the cell phone. Her head spun. She wasn't sure she'd heard correctly. "Johnny? But he's…he's dead."

"Do not insult me. You know where he is. Bring him to me and your daughter will be returned to you. Do anything other than exactly what I tell you and you will never see your child again."

Paige's mouth went dry and her heart squeezed with pain. "I don't know where he is. I haven't seen him in years. I thought he was dead." She took a sobbing breath. "I just want my baby back."

"Then you know what you have to do."

"You can't do this! I'll…I'll go to the police."

An ominous laugh crackled through the phone. "Don't be stupid, Paige. If you go to the police, or tell anyone at all, I'll know. And little girls are so very small and fragile.''

Paige could hardly force breath through her constricted throat. ''No, wait. I'll do it. Just don't hurt her.''

How was she going to do this? She had no idea. She vowed to tear the city apart brick by brick if she had to, to save her child.

The voice went cold with impatience. ''Whether she's hurt is entirely up to you. I'll talk with you again soon.''

''Please! Don't hang up! I have to hear her voice. I have to know she's all right.''

She heard a sigh on the other end of the line, then a curt command. Her heart beat faster. Her pulse pounded in her ears.

''Mom—''

The word was cut off short, but it was Katie. Paige wanted to scream into the phone, but Katie's voice was small and scared, so she bent all her will to sounding calm.

''Katie? Hi, sweetie. I love you.''

''Mom, come get me—''

''Oh, Katie, I'm trying to. Be brave, honey.''

''Nice sentiment, Paige.''

Her throat ached with the need to cry. ''Katie,'' she mouthed soundlessly.

''But you don't have time for sentiment. Your daughter's time runs out when the cell phone battery runs out.''

''Wait! What do I do if I find him?''

''You don't worry about that.''

''But how will I get in touch with…?'' Paige realized she was speaking to a dead phone. She dropped it as if it were hot and stared at it, wringing her hands.

"Katie," she whispered hoarsely, then forced herself to take a deep breath. "Okay. I can do this. Think."

She paced back and forth clenching and unclenching her fists as she wrestled with the panic that threatened to overwhelm her. She worked to gain control of her whirling thoughts.

The picture. The picture with Johnny's signature on it. Paige felt a minuscule flutter of hope. She'd call Sally and find out about the picture.

Grabbing the cell phone, she punched buttons, but nothing happened. She looked at it. The little display screen was black. Not even the time or the signal showed. She shook it and punched buttons again.

What was wrong with the stupid phone? It was like the keys were stuck. She wanted to throw it, but instead she clutched it to her chest. It was her only link to her baby.

A vise of terror clamped around her heart. Katie was in danger and she didn't know where she was, or how to get in touch with her.

Paige forced herself not to give in to terror and grief. She had to think. What could she do? She stared at the silent phone. She tried to remember everything the kidnapper had said, but her brain wouldn't work right.

Oh God, she needed to hear Katie's voice again. If she could just hear her, she could be sure she was all right.

Her tape recorder! She had a minirecorder that she used to dictate notes about her social work clients.

She could record the calls. Maybe she could somehow use the information to find Katie.

She ran into her bedroom and grabbed the little tape recorder off her bedside table. Having it didn't do much to calm her growing panic, though. It didn't solve her biggest problem. She thought about the voice's demand. She had to find Johnny Yarbrough.

How was she going to find a dead man?

Chapter Two

Paige stood in front of yet another tiny, musty shop. She'd been inside dozens of similar shops today, up and down the streets near the docks.

She'd taken a cab back to Sally's place last night, but Sally hadn't been available. She'd gone off with a gentleman friend, according to her housekeeper. But she'd left the drawing in case Paige came by.

Frustration and fear had Paige's muscles wound as tight as springs. She hadn't slept. She hadn't eaten. Now it was almost dark and she still hadn't found the right shop.

She wasn't sure how much longer she could last. Nausea gnawed at her insides and she couldn't stop trembling as she clutched the cell phone in one hand and the small, framed sketch in the other.

What if she did something wrong and those people hurt Katie? What if the artist wasn't Johnny?

What if he was?

The cell phone rang.

Paige jumped and almost dropped it. She jabbed the one button that worked. "Katie?"

"It's been sixteen hours, Paige. That battery won't last forever."

"Wait!" she cried, fumbling in her pocket for her tape recorder. The phone went dead.

Paige froze. Were they watching her? Had they seen her pull the tape recorder out of her pocket? She looked up and down the street, the hairs on her neck prickling, the weight on her chest making it hard to breathe.

She didn't need the faceless voice to tell her how long it had been. She knew exactly, down to the second. It had taken all her will not to go to the police. It had taken all her strength to make it this far. The only thing that had kept her going was Katie.

This was for Katie.

Forcing her leaden limbs to work, she entered the shop.

The interior was dark after the bright sunlight outside. The odor of incense and mildew swirled around her. Exotic fabrics draped the walls and spilled over counters and chairs. On a shelf stood a number of apothecary bottles labeled with odd names like wolfsbane and maidenhair.

A table held an ominous collection of straw and rag dolls, some with long, pearl-tipped pins stuck in them.

On the main counter was a drawing held flat by a yardstick. Like the one in her hands, it was deceptively simple, no more than a few perfectly executed lines. An old pier with a seagull perched on a board was in the foreground, with a hint of mist-shrouded sea behind.

She peered closer, squinting in the dimness. The date was three months ago. Her heart sped up. The signature was the same.

Paige caught the edge of the counter as relief sent

dizzying blood rushing to her head. Finally, she'd found the right place.

Beads clattered as a dark woman in a yellow turban stepped into the room. "Ah, *c'est vous.*"

Paige started. "What?"

"It is you. From the drawings."

Paige studied the thin, brightly dressed woman. Her eyes, enormous and black in her dark face, reflected wisdom and sympathy, along with a hint of amusement. Maybe she would help her.

Paige held out the framed sketch. "I must find the artist."

"Ah, everyone comes to Tante Yvette seeking the mysterious artist."

"You mean other people have been asking about him?" Her fingers tightened around the cell phone in her pocket. "Who?"

"Two men," the woman spat. "Rough. Stupid."

"Did you tell them?"

The woman laughed and the sound echoed through the little shop like a wind chime. "It is not my place to tell secrets."

"I have to find him. Please." Paige heard the desperation in her voice, the rising panic.

The turbaned woman shook her head and waved a thin hand. A dozen or more bracelets jangled. "Perhaps he does not wish to be found."

Despair clutched at Paige like punishing fingers. "Who is he? You have to tell me. My daughter...." She stopped.

If you tell anyone...your daughter is so small and fragile.

The jangling bracelets stilled. "Your daughter?"

Paige shook her head. "Never mind. I have to find the artist. It's important."

"Many things are important. For this artist, perhaps not being found is important."

"Please don't talk to me in riddles," Paige begged. "If you won't help me, just say so. I don't have much time." She thought of Katie, of what the kidnappers might be doing to her.

Tante Yvette stared at her intently. "Time? For what?"

Paige shook her head, but before she could speak, a noise outside startled her. She clutched the frame closer and didn't breathe.

"You are afraid," the woman said. "Tell Tante Yvette who frightens you."

Paige shook her head. "I can't. They—they'll know."

Tante Yvette looked thoughtful for a moment. "You are the girl in the picture, *non?*"

Paige looked down at the carefully drawn eyes, the exquisite perfection of the few lines that formed the shoulders, neck and hair. Then she stared at the signature and the date.

The answer was unbelievable, but for Katie's sake she prayed it was true.

She met Tante Yvette's gaze. "Yes."

The older woman nodded. "Come with me."

She led Paige behind the beaded curtain into an apartment that connected to another apartment, then another. As they encountered other people and stepped around furniture, Tante Yvette gestured or spoke in what was probably French. No one said a word to Paige.

Finally they walked through a crowded storeroom

to a heavy door. "Go out this door and turn right. Stay behind the buildings. Go to the hotel and ask the old drunk."

"But where are you sending me?"

"You want to find the artist?"

Paige nodded, her head pounding with exhaustion.

"You are the girl in the picture?"

She nodded again.

"Then go."

Tante Yvette opened the door and Paige stepped out. She turned back. "Please be careful," she whispered to the woman who was helping her. "They're dangerous."

Tante Yvette nodded. "Go."

The alley was shadowed and dark, and held the stench of too many garbage bins. Paige walked quickly, swallowing the nausea that swirled in her empty stomach.

Any minute the phone would ring and the voice would tell her she'd lost her chance to ever see her daughter again.

She had no idea if she were doing the right thing. She certainly didn't know why Tante Yvette had helped her. Or even *if* she had. She could be walking into a trap.

But nothing that happened to her could be worse than losing Katie. If there was any chance this alley would lead to Johnny, she had to take it.

Johnny. She shook her head. It was impossible. Beyond belief. But what if it was true? What if Johnny Yarbrough was still alive?

Exploring the answer to that question was more than Paige's battered emotions could take. If this mysterious artist was Johnny, she was about to trade his life for her daughter's.

For his daughter's.

She couldn't think about that. All she could think about was Katie.

Expecting any minute to feel a rough hand grabbing her, or to hear the cell phone ring, Paige continued down the dark, stinking alley.

Sitting on the front steps of the hotel was an old black man dressed in a dingy shirt and tie, wearing a jacket that left his bony wrists bare.

Paige walked cautiously up to him, glancing around.

The old man studied her through rheumy eyes.

She held out the picture. "Do you know where he is?"

"You're the girl," the old man said.

She nodded. "Yes. I'm the girl."

"So his past has come to meet him." The old man yawned and pulled a bottle out of his pocket, then took a long swig. "I reckon Jay wouldn't have put that picture out there 'less he was looking for an answer."

"Jay? His name is Jay?" She thought of the monogram with its three initials and the signature on the drawing.

JAY.

He nodded and stood, wiping his mouth. "Down at the end of the hall. Don't you do him bad, you understand?"

Paige found herself answering reflexively. "No, sir."

The old man chuckled and walked away.

She ran up the steps into a hall lit by dim bulbs

that made pale circles of light on the floor. Paige walked down the empty corridor; her sneakers were soundless on the hardwood.

The last door was room twelve. She shifted the picture to her right hand and wiped her left one on her jeans. Behind this scarred wooden door might be the man who had left her alone, who had broken her heart.

The one man who could save her daughter.

She was trembling so much that she could hardly make a fist to knock.

She lifted her hand.

JAY WELLCOME JERKED at the sound of the rapping on his door. The charcoal broke in his suddenly tense fingers. Nobody ever knocked on his door except the landlord, and today was not the first of the month.

He set the sketchbook aside and stood. A glance told him the window opposite the door was unlocked. It had been almost three years since he'd woken up wounded and alone, with no idea of who he was or what had happened to him. And still he remained always aware of everything around him.

He waited, wondering when whoever had failed to kill him before would try again.

Satisfied that his escape route through the window and out to his deceptively battered car was clear, he pulled a T-shirt over his head, brushed his hair back with a quick gesture, and stepped over to the door.

He listened for a second, but didn't hear anything. Cautiously, balanced on the balls of his feet, poised for fight or flight, he opened the door.

And found himself staring at the girl who haunted his dreams.

He almost ran; almost slammed the door. He wasn't ready for this.

He'd let Tante Yvette and Old Mose talk him into putting the sketches out there. He'd been skeptical, torn between a yearning to pull himself out of the dead zone where he'd existed nameless and lost for so long, and the fear of being found. He'd spent the past three years working on the oil rigs, and always, always, looking over his shoulder.

He really hadn't expected a response. He hadn't expected to sell a drawing. And he certainly hadn't expected this.

He stood there clutching the doorknob, staring at her.

Although the resemblance was obvious, she was older than the girl in his dreams. She was a woman. A beautiful woman.

The wheat-colored hair he remembered as short and shaggy was long, smooth, and woven into some kind of intricate braid that hung down her back.

She was smaller than he'd thought she'd be. The top of her head barely reached his chin.

The girl in his dreams was thin. This woman had curves where a woman should have curves. The eyes were the same though. Familiar gold-flecked green eyes that seemed sunken and sad in a face that was no longer round and blushing with youth. It was pale.

He realized it was getting paler.

She whispered a name.

He stiffened. He was being way too careless. The shock of seeing her had caught him off guard. Straightening, he took a step backward and tried to make sense of her words.

''What did you say?'' he snapped.

She clutched a small, framed picture to her chest. If possible, her face lost even more color. She looked as if she were seeing a ghost.

"Johnny? What happened to you?"

Johnny? The name meant nothing to him. Did she know him?

Without thinking about the possible consequences he reached out and grabbed her arm, pulling her inside the room. With a lightning-fast glance into the hall, he pushed the door shut.

She backed away from him, up against the heavy wooden door. "What are you doing?"

Jay studied her. Her pale face showed a strength of character, a wisdom that wasn't in the young innocent face he'd drawn.

The eyes though, were hauntingly familiar. The only difference was these eyes were filled with terror, and they hadn't left his face since he'd opened the door.

"Who are you?" he demanded.

Shock darkened her gaze and lifted her delicate brows for an instant. Then she seemed to shrink, and something changed in her. A tension, or anticipation, drained out of her, leaving her seeming even smaller. Her enormous green-and-gold eyes closed and she shook her head slowly, once.

When she looked at him again, her expression was carefully blank, although the rigid set of her spine had not relaxed at all.

"I almost didn't recognize you either," she said tightly, "but it's impossible to forget those sapphire-colored eyes of yours."

Johnny stared at her, panic shearing his breath as

he wondered if he should be relieved or worried that someone had finally recognized him.

Paige swallowed hard, hanging on to control with as much force as she hung on to the picture. He was so different. This was not the boy she had fallen in love with. This wasn't the frustrated young artist who was so intimidated by his father he couldn't even bring a girlfriend home to meet him without getting permission first.

This was a man.

A strong, hard-eyed, capable man with calluses on his artist's fingers and a scar that parted his hair and lent a cynical lift to one dark eyebrow.

Paige's gaze traveled over shoulders that she was sure had not been this broad, down the front of his T-shirt to the faded jeans that molded over long powerful thighs, then back up to his face.

It could be someone else's face, harsh, scored by years and darkened by the sun. But there was no mistaking the eyes. They were the same brilliant blue eyes that had regarded her so tenderly as he told her how much he loved her. Now they blazed with startling intensity in his tanned face.

She wasn't sure what was going on behind those familiar eyes. He watched her warily, all senses alert, like a cat watches an unknown threat. His taut, muscled body was perfectly balanced, his hands loose but open and ready at his sides, his gaze never leaving her face.

"It's Paige," she ventured, wanting to cry because she had to remind the only man she'd ever loved of her name. She tried a smile. "Paige Reynolds."

He frowned. He frightened her, this familiar stranger who stood in a dingy, sordid hotel room and acted like he'd never seen her before today, but whom she knew without a doubt was the father of her daughter.

Katie! Searing loss and chilling fear met with stormy force inside her. Her head reeled and she swayed.

"Are you all right?" Johnny asked, reaching toward her.

She pressed her lips together to gain control of her emotions.

Hold on. This is for Katie's sake.

She nodded stiffly.

"Good." His voice was cold. "Now what are you doing here, and what did you call me?"

Paige lifted her chin. "I called you Johnny. Johnny Yarbrough. It's your name."

He didn't move a muscle, but she felt his increased tension like an aura surrounding him. She saw the vein that beat in his temple, saw the infinitesimal tightening of his wide, generous mouth.

"Johnny Yarbrough," he repeated, his voice no more than a croaking whisper. His lips barely moved. "Yarbrough." His mouth closed grimly and a muscle jumped in his jaw. He winced, touching the side of his head.

Paige stared at him. He was acting so strange. "Actually," she said wryly, "I guess that would be John Andrew Yarbrough. You never told me who you really were."

His eyes never left her face, but she had the sense he wasn't looking at her at all. His fingers slipped through his sun-kissed brown hair, and then went back to his temple.

"Johnny?"

He shook his head, looking confused.

"I don't understand. What's the matter with you? You act like you—"

The truth hit her like a wrecking ball. In one explosive instant, everything Paige had pinned her hopes on crashed down around her.

As unbelievable as it was, it explained everything. Why no one had ever found a body. Why he'd never returned to his rightful place in his father's business. Why he looked so bewildered.

"Oh my God," she whispered, stunned.

Her daughter's life was at stake, and the only man who could save her didn't know who he was. Telling him he had a daughter would mean nothing to him.

"You don't remember." Her numb lips formed the words, hoping he would deny them, but knowing he wouldn't.

He couldn't.

He sent her a terrible, haunted glance, then turned away.

She stared at his bowed back, watched his bicep flex as he massaged his temple.

Her brain rejected the idea. It couldn't be true. She couldn't allow it to be true.

"I need your help." She took a step toward him. "Look at me," she pleaded. "Look at this."

He angled his head, and the muscles in his back rippled the white cotton of his T-shirt. Then he half turned, his long lashes shadowing his eyes.

She held up the drawing. "You drew me. We were together here, in New Orleans, seven years ago. You can't tell me you don't remember that."

He faced her, his jaw set, his eyes bleak. He shrugged. "I don't remember that."

"You have to. If you don't remember me, surely you remember being kidnapped?"

His eyes narrowed. He took a step toward her. "I was kidnapped?"

Paige gasped and forced down the panic that bubbled up into her throat. "Of course. Three years ago. It was all over the news. The ransom note demanded two million dollars. After weeks and weeks, your wallet covered with your blood was found in a stolen car out by Chef Menteur Highway. You were—presumed dead." She couldn't believe he didn't remember anything.

"Your father begged the kidnappers not to harm you. He offered twice the ransom if they'd just let you go." Paige stopped to take a shaky breath.

"Your father gave them the money. Nobody understood why they killed…" Her voice died on the word and she stared at his familiar, alien face.

There was pain there, and a kind of bewildered disbelief. But she also saw a spark of interest, and something that almost broke her heart. For one naked second, she saw hope reflected in his eyes.

He wasn't lying. He really didn't remember.

Oh, Johnny. What did they do to you?

She caught herself and shook her head. She didn't have time for sentiment or pity. She had to save her child. It was her only reason for being here. Her only reason for living now.

Once she'd thought she knew him better than she knew herself. She'd have staked her life on his honesty. But he'd promised her he was coming back for her and he hadn't.

He'd lied to her then. Was he lying now?

But why would he be here in this seedy hotel instead of living the wealthy life he was born to? Why would he draw her picture then deny he knew her?

"Do you expect me to believe you don't remember any of that?" Her gaze fell on the scar that started at his hairline and furrowed along a couple of inches, like a carefully combed part.

At the same time he lifted his hand and touched it. "All I know is somebody tried to kill me. Who kidnapped me?"

"I don't know." She swallowed, "We weren't together then. We last saw each other seven years ago."

He reached out and took the picture from her hands and looked at it, then at her, searching her eyes as if he hoped to find the answers he sought there.

"How long did we know each other?"

She shrugged and twisted the ends of her braid, painfully aware of the time ticking by. "About six weeks."

Long enough to create a beautiful child who was out there, held captive by dangerous strangers. What if they hurt her?

"We knew each other for six weeks seven years ago," he muttered, more to himself than to her. "So why do you haunt my dreams?"

"Why do I what?"

He tossed the picture on the bed, on top of other similar sketches. A few were of her.

He looked up, and for a second the caution and doubt in his face changed to a yearning so strong, Paige felt its pull like a fishing line, reeling her in. Then he blinked and it was gone.

"So you knew me once," he said quietly, a bitter longing rising up like bile inside him as he stared at the drawings, those pathetic attempts to capture the visions that streaked through his brain when the headaches hit him.

He looked at the woman whose face haunted him. "I assume you traced me through that picture to Tante Yvette. She sent you here?"

She nodded.

Tante Yvette had trusted her. The strange dark woman claimed to know things, to be able to read minds. He hoped she was right this time.

He studied the lovely, hauntingly familiar face of Paige Reynolds for a moment. The glint of panic in her golden-green eyes and the tension in her shoulders told him she was a hairsbreadth from losing control.

But as familiar as she was, he didn't know her and his small store of memories made it hard for him to trust anyone, even someone Tante Yvette believed.

"What do you want from me?" he asked coldly.

He winced at the unguarded hope that flared in her green eyes. "They've got my daughter," she whispered, clenching her fists.

He hadn't expected that. "Your daughter? Who does?"

She shook her head. "I don't know. But they told me to find you."

At her words, Jay tensed. Almost unconsciously he shifted his weight to the balls of his feet, alert, prepared for anything.

"Were you followed?" he snapped.

Her brow furrowed briefly. She looked down at her fist, clenched in her jacket pocket, then over her shoulder at the door. "Yes."

He heard a noise behind her. "Look out!"

Wood splintered and the door flew open, hurling her into his arms. The breath hissed out of her and she squealed in pain. He tossed her back toward the bed, hoping to get her out of harm's way, as the two men attacked him.

He struggled, fighting dirty, aiming for the groin, the kidneys, the nose, any vulnerable spot. He'd learned how to fight the hard way out on the oil rigs.

One man was beefier, thicker than the other. Jay concentrated on his face.

He punched, felt something crunch, then drove an elbow behind him into the smaller man's solar plexus.

A fist connected with his jaw. He stumbled. The small man pinned his arms behind him and Beefy reared back a fist, prepared to punch him in the stomach.

Jay used the momentum of the small man's grip to lift his feet. He drove them into Beefy's stomach, pushing himself backward at the same time.

Beefy fell. The smaller man huffed as Jay's weight pinned him against the wall. Jay turned, jerking his arms clear, then smashed the guy's nose with his forearm.

When he looked back at Beefy, the big man was trying to regain his feet. Jay kicked him solidly in the groin.

Both men were down for the moment. The smaller man's nose was pouring blood. Beefy was doubled over with pain. But they'd recover fast.

Jay wiped his mouth with the back of his hand, barely noting his own blood as he rushed around the bed.

He bent over the woman. She was unconscious, or nearly so. When he slid one hand under her back and the other under her knees, she whimpered.

"Sorry," he whispered, afraid she was injured but

knowing he didn't have time to find out. He hefted her, absently noting how small she was, and took her out through the French doors. He kneed the doors closed and glanced inside. The two men were beginning to stir.

Hurrying to the old sedan he kept in tiptop shape for just this purpose, he opened the passenger door and carefully set her inside. He quickly and awkwardly fastened her seat belt, then ran around the car, got in, grabbed the keys from under the mat, cranked it and took off.

Chapter Three

Not until Jay reached the edge of the city did he relax his hunched shoulders and breathe a bit easier. They'd made it, for now. The whole process, from the moment the brutes had broken in the door, slamming the woman forward into his arms, until he'd cranked the car, had probably taken no longer than five minutes, eight at the most. Unless there had been a third guy watching the alley, Jay was sure he'd lost them.

As he took a right off the main road, he glanced over at his unconscious passenger. She was limp and still, her face shadowed, her braid draped across her shoulder and over her breast.

For a split second, his eyes lingered there, where the rope of wheat-colored hair rose and fell with the slight movement of her breathing.

Pulling his eyes back to the road, he drove the familiar route to his safe house. He'd always felt vaguely foolish about the elaborate escape plan he'd devised, but waking up with a bullet wound and no memory tended to make a guy paranoid.

Obviously, some deeply buried part of his brain had remembered enough of what had happened to him to keep his survival skills intact.

He took a long breath and thought about the last few moments. What he'd always feared had happened, with a twist, and now he was running away from thugs with an unconscious woman beside him.

Not just any woman either. The woman whose face haunted him, whose image he'd tried time and again to capture.

He searched her face. There was no doubt in his mind. She was the girl in his drawings. The girl in his head.

She'd said they'd known each other years ago. Had they been lovers? Was that why her face was the clearest memory he'd managed to glean from his battered brain?

She'd called him Johnny. Implied he'd come from serious money, and that he'd been kidnapped and presumed dead. Obviously whoever had wanted him dead back then still did, and they'd kidnapped an innocent child to find him.

Kidnapped.

Clenching his jaw against the panic that washed over him, he forced himself to think about it, testing the idea in his brain. It made sense. Was that why he was so damned afraid of the dark? Why the headaches that assaulted him yielded up such a suffocating claustrophobia?

He wiped sweat off his face, tongued his split lip, and waited for his pulse to slow as the panic finally eased.

Maybe he should have taken the woman to the police. Maybe he should have left her there with the thugs. It wasn't impossible that she'd deliberately led them to him.

Shaking his head he pushed damp hair off his forehead; neither of those choices were an option. He'd recognized her the instant he opened the door, as soon as he'd looked into her eyes. He'd always known those eyes were green and gold. He'd known her chin stuck up pugnaciously when she was mad.

Somehow, somewhere, in his malfunctioning brain, he knew she had once been the most important person in the world to him.

She still was, because if she'd known him seven years ago, then she was the one person who could help him regain his lost memories, the one person in the world he might be able to trust.

A cell phone rang. He jumped, startled, the car swerving under his unsteady hands.

"What the hell?" It must be hers.

She whimpered and stirred.

Jay tried to ignore the phone, but he couldn't. If he was going to make any sense out of what was happening, he had to have every bit of information available, including who was calling this mysterious woman from his past.

He reached out and felt around for the phone, doing his best to ignore her rounded woman's body. His mouth quirked and he shifted uncomfortably as he searched blindly, keeping his eyes on the road. It had been a little too long since he'd touched a woman.

The ringing continued. She moaned, saying something, but didn't wake.

He pulled over to the side of the road and took the car out of gear. He searched her pockets. Finally, on the fourth ring, his hand closed around the hard plastic case in her jacket pocket. He pulled it out and looked at it. The caller ID was blocked.

After hesitating for a brief second, he pressed the answer button and listened.

Just then Paige stirred and lifted her head. She blinked and moved, then froze, gasping with pain. Her wide, terrified eyes glittered, pleading with him in the darkness.

"Give me the phone," she whispered, her words strained and breathless.

"Who is this?" the voice on the other end of the phone demanded.

He didn't speak. There was something in the background, some sound that seemed familiar. He listened intently, his head beginning to throb, as the voice spoke.

"Paige? Don't play games with me."

Paige reached into her pocket with her right hand, moaning involuntarily as she moved. She pulled out a minitape recorder and turned it on, then tried to take the cell phone with her left hand, but she couldn't manage it.

She had a tape recorder. He was impressed.

The voice from the phone called her name again.

Without a word, Jay held the phone up to her ear.

"Katie," she sobbed dryly, pressing her head tightly against the phone. He held it steady for her.

"I'm sorry. I...dropped the phone. Where's Katie?" As if just remembering the tape recorder, she held it close to the cell phone. She listened for a moment, then cut her eyes over at Jay, looking away when he met her gaze. "Yes. I found him. You should know. You had me followed."

She listened, breathing in short bursts. She was obviously in pain.

He pushed away the easy compassion that rose in

him. She was negotiating with these people, using him as a bargaining chip.

"I swear. I will. You just tell me where and when. But I have to talk to Katie. I won't do anything for you unless you prove to me she's all right."

Jay glanced at her pale, pinched face. He was surprised at the strength of will in her voice. She was obviously in pain, judging by the way she avoided moving her left arm. He was pretty sure she had a dislocated or broken shoulder. He hoped to hell it wasn't broken.

"Katie, honey? Hi."

Jay held the phone, feeling her inner struggle. He could tell she wanted to drop the tape recorder and press the phone as close as she could to her ear. He had to give her credit for having the presence of mind to record the call.

He didn't look at her, offering her as much illusion of privacy as he could. Her voice was thick with tears, and at the same time deliberately and pitifully cheerful.

"Are you okay, sweetie? They're being nice to you?" She paused, and took a long, shaky breath. "It's dark at night? Oh, Katie. I know you don't like the dark." Her voice quivered. "But remember what I told you? God wraps us up in the soft dark night to keep us safe."

Jay winced. They were holding the child in the dark. An echo of the panic that had seized him earlier rippled through him again. He rubbed his temple where a headache was starting.

"You have Ugly Afghan? I'm so glad. Keep it wrapped tight and pretend it's my arms, okay?"

Jay heard her voice almost break. She swallowed

audibly. "Be brave, okay?" Paige continued. "No, I know you don't like canned soup, but you eat it and stay strong. We'll have p-pizza real soon, okay, hon—"

She stopped abruptly, listening. Jay glanced at her. Her face was still pale, her lips white with tension. "I understand," she grated. "If you hurt her, I swear I'll—"

She slumped. "They hung up."

Jay glanced at the phone. Nothing showed on the display window except the battery indicator and the digital clock.

She took it away from him.

After he'd pulled back onto the road, Jay glanced at her. "So your plan is to trade me for your daughter?"

She looked at him, her eyes dark and haunted, but her chin held high. "What do you think? You're a grown man. She's just a baby."

Jay allowed himself a wry smile at his earlier thought that he might be able to trust her.

"They told me they'd kill her. They're keeping her in the dark. Katie hates the dark." Her voice broke. "Will you help me?"

"How do you think I can help? I don't know you. I sure don't know them. What do you want me to do, offer myself to them?"

She met his gaze. "The Johnny I knew would have done anything in his power to protect a child."

Jay's heart slammed into his chest with the force of a blow. *The Johnny she'd known.*

"And you think I'm that man?" he asked. The effort of holding hope at bay inside him harshened his voice.

She held his gaze for a moment, her eyes wide and haunted. Then she shook her head. "I don't know."

An odd pang of hurt and disappointment sliced through his heart at her words.

It wasn't hard for him to imagine how frightened and alone the child must feel. Ever since he'd awakened, wounded and lost, with murky water closing over his head, he'd been haunted by nightmarish visions of unrelenting darkness and suffocating panic.

But he'd also been comforted by the vision of a beautiful young woman, this woman. If he weren't careful, she could make him believe in himself.

She moved to put the phone back into her pocket, and cried out softly when she moved.

"That was smart of you to record the call."

She didn't say anything.

Jay turned left, into what looked like a part of the swamp but was really a road. As many times as he'd driven this route, daylight, nighttime, rain, he still had trouble navigating the deep, narrow ruts.

Precisely two-tenths of a mile later, he turned again and pulled up in front of a broken-down cabin.

His safe house. It was ironic that he was here with this woman he didn't remember who wanted him to give himself up for her child.

Paige winced in pain as the car came to an abrupt stop in front of an old abandoned shack. Ever since she'd regained consciousness and realized she was in a car with Johnny driving, she'd felt every bump in the road through her hurt shoulder. She couldn't move it, and the pain radiating down her arm and up her neck was excruciating.

When the car stopped, she raised her head, biting back a moan. "Where are we?"

"Don't worry about it."

"Well, you can't stop here. We have to find Katie—" She paused, realizing she had no idea where to even start looking.

Her plan had ended at Johnny's door. She hadn't considered what she would do after she found him. Now pain and exhaustion were making it hard to think.

Johnny came around and opened the passenger door.

"No, wait. Please. We have to go back. My daughter's out there. They have her locked in the dark."

"We can't do anything until we see how badly you're hurt. You're just going to have to trust me." He leaned down and looked at her. "Can you stand?"

"Of course I can." Paige tried to move, but the seat belt held her trapped. She fumbled with the catch, her shoulder screaming with agony.

"Hold on. Let me."

Johnny leaned over her and placed his large, callused hand on top of hers, stilling her desperate movements. She pulled her hand away and sat stiffly as he quickly and efficiently unbuckled the seat belt.

Then he slid his arms gently behind her back and under her knees.

"What are you doing?"

"Just let me carry you. You could have other injuries. You could have hit your head. You don't need to be walking."

Paige closed her eyes against the expectation of agonizing pain, and was surprised at the tenderness with which he lifted her into his arms.

She allowed herself to be carried. There was an awkward moment when he wrestled the cabin door open, jostling her shoulder, but soon he deposited her on a couch and went around lighting lanterns.

As light filtered into the corners of the room, Paige took in her surroundings. The shack was old and built of rough-hewn wood. The furnishings were sparse and stark.

At one end of the room were a wood stove and a counter with shelves that held a few plates and cups and pots. At the other end was a dark curtain that she figured must hide a sleeping area.

There was almost nothing to indicate that anyone lived here. But when Johnny lit the last lantern, Paige saw the sketches tacked to the wall in front of the couch.

These were dark slashes of charcoal, like nightmares brought to life under the artist's pencil. Her heart twisted in compassion. How many times had he sat here, trying to make sense of the pieces of memory his mind fed him?

Her fertile imagination made her wonder if these were visions of his kidnapping. They evoked all her darkest emotions. Anger, fear, even hatred.

She couldn't even imagine what he must have gone through. If the drawings were any indication, the place where they'd held him must have been a dark and frightening place.

She looked away, fear welling up in her throat until she thought she would scream. If they were holding Katie in a place like that...

"Can't you hurry?" she asked, struggling to stand. Her knees collapsed beneath her as she reeled at the pain. "We have to find Katie."

Johnny tossed the matches down on a table beside

the last lamp he'd lit. "I need some light to look at your shoulder."

"Fine. You've got light. Do something. My daughter is out there."

He walked over to the kitchen area.

She gritted her teeth in frustration. "Aren't you listening to me?"

He stuck a cup under her nose, a cup filled almost to the brim with a dark liquid. The sweet, hot smell of brandy hit her. "What's that for?"

"Drink up. You'll need something to numb the pain."

"I can't be drunk. I haven't eaten all day. What if they call?"

"I'm sure if they call you'll manage. Now drink it." His harsh voice brooked no argument.

Paige shot him a venomous glance and reluctantly took the chipped cup. Her throbbing shoulder was sending waves of nauseating pain through her. The idea of stopping it for a little while was seductive.

She drank. The fiery stuff gagged her. She coughed, then drank some more. When she'd managed to down about half the cup, he took it and set it aside, then sat down beside her.

She tensed.

"Why did these people send you to find me? Why would they think you knew where I was?" he asked as he laid his hand on her shoulder.

Paige didn't want to answer that question. She was stuck here, dependent on him. She had to have his help. If she told him the truth about why they'd kidnapped Katie, he might not believe her. He might not want to help her.

"That's a good question," she said, hoping he'd drop the subject.

"I'm listening if you want to give me a good answer," he said, smiling slightly. "Tell me about us." His hand gently traced the line of her shoulder, running over the place that hurt so badly, the place where she knew something was wrong.

"Us," she repeated wryly. She was feeling woozy from the brandy, but at least every breath wasn't total agony now.

"You said we met seven years ago."

"In Jackson Square. I was on my way to work. I went to school during the day and worked at night."

Johnny was feeling her shoulder with both hands now, his touch at once familiar and alien. They were Johnny's gentle, caring fingers, but back then his hands had been soft.

Now rough calluses scraped her skin, and his arms were bronzed by the sun. He was different.

It was a very interesting difference.

"You asked if you could draw me." She smiled sleepily. "You said I had a classic face."

"You do."

She lifted heavy eyelids to find his gaze roaming over her eyes and nose and mouth. It felt like gentle fingers tracing her features. His lashes shadowed his eyes as his gaze lingered on her suddenly dry lips. She licked them.

He frowned, then blinked. "I don't think your shoulder is completely dislocated. That's good," he said, putting a hand on either side of her shoulder, where it hurt so bad.

"Have you ever done this before?" Paige didn't like the way her words were coming out. They were slow and slurred. But she did like the way Johnny's hands felt. The warmth of his roughened fingers was comforting. They seemed to soak the pain right out of her.

"Let's say I have some experience. Tell me what happened after I drew you."

His hands were gently massaging her shoulder. It hurt, but not as much as moving it herself did.

"I was seventeen. You may have been twenty-one." She was back there again, sitting in the hot sun during the day while his talented hands created magic on paper. Then at night in her apartment, those hands created magic on her body. She closed her eyes as the memories stirred sweet yearnings inside her. "We fell in love."

She had trusted him, but he'd broken her heart.

"You promised me you'd come back for me. You gave me this ring." She started to hold up her left hand, but Johnny was squeezing her shoulder.

"I waited and waited. I watched out the window for days."

The old familiar ache began in her chest. "But you never came back." She licked her lips and let her eyes drift shut. "Never came back."

Paige's gently slurred voice cut a deep furrow into Jay's heart. Something shifted inside him. The painful emptiness that he'd carried around ever since he'd woken up alone began to throb.

She'd waited for him. And he hadn't come back. She took a short sobbing breath. "Now Katie is out there. Oh, God. What if we never find her?"

"We'll find her," he murmured, concentrating on her shoulder. He hoped he could get it back into place without harming her. He'd watched the doc on the oil rigs do it a time or two.

Paige's voice penetrated his thoughts. "You never

told me your family was rich as Croesus. You were just Johnny Yarbrough.''

Jay stilled. "Rich as Croesus?"

"Sure." Paige giggled again. "Yarbrough Shipping. Tons of money. More than enough to pay a two-million-dollar ransom. But they don't want a ransom. Just you." She took a sobbing breath.

"Just hang on a minute, Paige." Jay got ready to slip her shoulder back into its socket. He knew the brandy wasn't going to help much. He tightened his grip and looked at her. Her eyes were drifting closed. She looked lovely and vulnerable.

He slipped his hand under her arm and lifted and pushed.

Paige shrieked, then fell, limp, into his arms. She'd passed out.

Grateful that she was out of pain for the moment, Jay sat there, his hands cradling her awkwardly, unused to the human contact, but strangely and deeply affected by the feel of her in his arms.

Her satiny skin, the delicate curve of her neck and the petal-soft line of her cheek called up sensations in him that he never remembered feeling.

Three years was a long time to be alone and lost.

On an impulse that he didn't want to examine too closely, he pulled her closer, burying his nose in her hair. An ache of longing twisted his insides.

Something felt so right about holding her, about breathing the faint scent of gardenias that clung to her and threatened to draw up memories which drifted away before he could catch them.

He didn't understand half of what was going on. Why would someone kidnap Paige's daughter and send her to find him? Who were these people who were after him?

But right now, with her in his arms, the biggest mystery to him was why he'd had her and ever let her go.

She was brave. She was beautiful. She evoked a fierce protective urge in him that made him want to slay dragons for her.

What kind of man had he been to walk away from her?

As badly as he craved information about his past, Jay wasn't sure he wanted to know the answer to that question. He wasn't sure he liked the man he'd been, the man who had left her alone.

She stirred, and he reluctantly set her away from him. He looked critically at her shoulder. Everything seemed to be in place.

"Oh wow," she muttered. "That hurt."

"Can you move it?" he asked gruffly.

Paige frowned and shook her head as if to clear it. She tentatively lifted her arm, wincing. "It's sore," she said, "but not hurting so much." She looked at him, her eyes heavy-lidded. "Thank you."

Jay gave her a quick nod and got up. "You need to sleep."

"No, we have to go find Katie."

"After you rest a while." He gently pushed her down and slid an old throw pillow under her head. "I need to think. If my family is rich as Croesus, maybe they can help us."

She sat up again. "We can't tell anybody," she insisted. "They'll hurt her." She stood and swayed, putting her hand to her head.

Jay wrapped his fingers around her upper arms. "Listen to me."

She glared up at him. Her eyes were sleepy but her chin was high.

"Knew I couldn't count on you. Should've told 'em you wouldn't care."

Her words stung him. He had no idea who he was or what he had done to her, but he was sure she hadn't deserved it.

"Okay, Paige. We'll do it your way. What's your plan?"

Her glare could have burned him. "Go find Katie."

He looked down at her. "Where do we start?"

She blinked. "We...I...don't know."

Jay wanted to pull her into his arms and comfort her. He wanted to tell her everything would be fine. But he knew he couldn't promise her that.

"Your fault, Johnny. Your fault. Why'd you run? They wanted you. I could have my baby back."

Fighting, running, protecting her, had all been instinct. Maybe he shouldn't have. Maybe he should have somehow subdued the two men and tried to find out some information.

He shook his head. He'd done the only thing he could do under the circumstances.

He set her back down on the couch and crouched in front of her. He touched her chin, forcing her to look at him. She opened blurry eyes.

"Listen to me. Do you want to go to the police? I'll take you."

"No! They said they'd kill her. No police!"

Jay studied her. "Okay. Then there's nothing we can do tonight. We're safe here."

"But she's not. She's alone." Her voice broke.

His heart ached for her, for her child. Nobody knew better than he did the true meaning of alone.

He pushed a silky strand of hair off her cheek. "I know. We'll go as soon as it's light. We'll figure out who these people are, and why they did this."

"You're a Yarbrough," Paige murmured. "Worth millions."

He looked at the woman whose face haunted his dreams and finally gathered the courage to ask the question that had been burning inside him ever since she'd first told him about her child.

"Why did they take your daughter?"

She bit her lip and stared off beyond him, her eyes slightly unfocused from the effects of the brandy.

"They—they wanted me to lead them to you."

Jay shook his head. There had to be something more. "But why you? Why *your* daughter?"

As soon as the words were out of his mouth, he knew. It was the only answer that made sense. He couldn't even form the thought to himself. His knowing was more visceral, subconscious, deeper than words.

Pain shot through his head, and he clenched his jaw to keep from running to escape the darkness and fear that danced across his vision.

"Paige?"

She looked down at her hands. "I guess they thought you'd cooperate."

He touched her chin, forcing it up with a finger that trembled. "And why would they think that?"

Slowly, she met his gaze. When she spoke, her words were almost soundless.

"Because she's your daughter too."

Chapter Four

"Well, you're certainly your father's daughter," Serena said, carefully avoiding a dusty wooden box and wrinkling her nose. The abandoned warehouse smelled as fishy and moldy as it had three years before.

She could almost feel dust and grime settling on her Versace dress. "Not only do you have his eyes, you have his irritating stubbornness."

The child flashed her sapphire-blue eyes at Serena and pulled the hideous orange-and-green afghan closer around her. "I'm my mom's daughter," she said, her little chin jutting up. "My daddy's gone."

Serena snorted. "Smart-mouthed too, Katie. Well, your daddy is not gone…yet."

"I want to talk to my mom." Katie's eyes glistened with tears.

Good. Serena was glad to see that the little girl was scared and upset. She needed information from her, information about her father.

Serena liked to keep the upper hand, and so far, her irritating stepson had twice managed to elude Leonard's men. She was anxious for them to take care of Johnny and Paige. Then she would arrange to be at some highly visible meeting or event while the child was eliminated.

"I want my mom. You can't keep me here. It's— it's against the law."

"Oh, really?" Serena laughed and took a long drag off her cigarette. "You're quite funny. Against the law indeed."

"It is. I saw it on TV. It's kidnapping. And they caught the man and they put him in jail."

"Smart like your father and grandfather, too," Serena muttered, then looked at her watch. Biting off a curse, she dialed a number on her cell phone.

"I'll be a little late for the board meeting," she said when her secretary answered. "Order in some pastries to go with the coffee and make my apologies."

She flipped off the phone.

"Now, Katie, I want you to answer some questions for me."

"I want to talk to my mom. Every time you come here, I get to talk to her."

Leonard stepped toward Katie. "Look here, kid. You talk to your mama after you answer questions. Get it?"

Katie shrank away from him.

"Leonard, you're frightening her," Serena said. "Now, Katie. Didn't I get you a night-light?"

"Mr. Martin did."

"Well, yes, but Mr. Martin works for me. And didn't he bring you pizza?"

"It was cold."

Leonard snorted.

Serena sighed impatiently. "I did all that for you. Now I want you to talk to me."

Serena inserted a cigarette into her holder and lit it, waving the smoke away.

"I don't want to. I want my mom."

Leonard stood over the little girl. "If you don't talk, you'll never see Mama again."

Katie blinked at him, and a fat tear rolled down her cheek. She looked at the cell phone Serena had laid on a nearby crate, then back at Serena.

"My m-mommy will call the police and they'll find you and put you in jail."

Serena checked her watch again. "Katie, I'm late for an appointment. I don't have time to play games." She took a puff off her cigarette and nodded at Leonard.

"Your mama ain't gonna go to the police, because if she does, she knows we'll kill you. You understand what that means?" He grinned.

Katie's eyes grew wide and another tear slipped from her eye. "Yes, sir."

"Now, Katie," Serena said, smiling at her. "I'm going to ask you some questions and you are going to give me some answers. If I like the answers, I'll let you talk to your mother for a minute. Agreed?"

"Okay," Katie said in a tiny voice.

JAY STOOD SHIRTLESS ON the stoop of his safe house and listened to water drip from the trees. The rain had only lasted a couple of hours. Thank goodness it hadn't disturbed Paige.

She'd needed to sleep. And he'd needed to think.

His fingers and scalp still tingled from the shock that had ripped through his body when she'd told him that her daughter was his.

His daughter.

It was what he'd expected her to say, but suspecting it was true and hearing her confirm it were two very different things.

He had a child. He had no memory of his own childhood, no memory of his parents, no experience or knowledge to give meaning to those four words.

He had a child.

Still, just saying them to himself filled a bit of the emptiness that ate at his insides.

What did his daughter look like? Was she blonde, like Paige? Did she have his odd dark-blue eyes? He tried to picture her, but all he could see was Paige.

Did Katie know he was her father?

And the biggest question, the one that would make all the difference was had he known Paige was pregnant when he'd left her?

Jay held out his hands to collect the runoff from the roof in his cupped palms, then splashed his face and pushed damp fingers through his hair. His skin tightened as cool droplets showered his shoulders and chest.

He wanted to know all that and more, wanted to make Paige tell him everything. But it was as if admitting to him that he was Katie's father had sapped the last of her energy. She'd slumped, exhausted, her body gone boneless.

So Jay had tucked an old blanket around her, and sat and watched as she slept restlessly, mumbling and whimpering. He was sure she was dreaming about Katie.

He hadn't been able to sleep. He'd been hyperalert, and the headache that had threatened all evening had pounded in his head.

It still did. He collected a bit more water and

splashed his eyes, wishing the coolness would relieve the searing pain.

He'd give Paige a little while longer, but then they needed to get going. He was so anxious to find answers that he could chew nails.

He wanted to examine Paige's apartment in case she'd missed a note or a clue. He wanted to talk to every person in the area who might have seen anyone with a little girl, and he wanted to search out information about the Yarbroughs.

The Yarbroughs. The people who were supposed to be his family. Yesterday morning he'd known nothing about his past. Now…his mind played back everything that had happened since he'd opened the door and seen her standing there.

He had so few memories he could call his own. Since he'd woken up with no memory of his previous life, he'd existed in a state of constant awareness, knowing that he was a wanted man. The bullet wound proved that.

Whether he was wanted by the police, or by an individual didn't matter. The threat was still there. What did matter to him was making sense out of the jumble of mixed-up memories inside his head.

Most of what was in his head from before was fractured and distorted, like trying to see something behind him through a broken mirror. The only images that had survived intact were her face and the suffocating darkness.

The best and the worst, he thought wryly.

He gathered another handful of water and splashed his face again, his palms scraping against a day's worth of stubble.

It frightened him how much he already depended

on her, how much he'd already risked on the chance that she might be able to give him back his memories. He'd always known his day of reckoning would come. But his wildest fantasies hadn't come close to the reality.

Now watery daylight was peeking through the moss-draped cypress trees and the swamp was waking up. Herons and egrets flapped their wings and began their day's work of finding food.

Here and there a splash or a rasping sound indicated that snakes and alligators and other swamp life were stirring.

Jay assessed the road. They couldn't delay any longer. It was going to be rough going because of last night's rain. The damn road carried a patina of mud even in dry weather. And that gumbo mud stuck to everything. Even the tires would get so coated and heavy the car could hardly move.

He grimaced as a breeze scattered raindrops from the overhanging limbs. If it started raining again, they'd be stuck. And he knew, as soon as Paige woke up she'd be the one chewing nails.

He turned to go inside to rouse her, but an odd noise stopped him.

He froze, listening. He didn't think it was a natural swamp sound. Could it be thunder? An alligator's roar?

He waited. There it was again. It was more of a buzz, far away but getting louder.

Car engine!

By the time the thought had fully formed, he was through the door. He grabbed Paige's jacket.

"Paige. Wake up."

She jumped. "Katie?"

He thrust her jacket at her. "Get up. Can you walk? We've got to get out of here."

"What time is it?"

"Get up!"

Paige pushed the blanket away and sat up, her eyes wide. She grabbed her jacket and put it on, moaning as she moved her left arm. "What's going on?"

Jay didn't answer her. He was busy arguing with himself about the advisability of what he was thinking. Unsure of his decision, he opened a tall kitchen cabinet and reached up into the back of the top shelf.

His fingers closed around cold metal as he pulled down the little Davis .380 he'd bought off a guy from the oil rigs. He felt around until he found the two extra magazines and stuck them in the pocket of his windbreaker. He slid the gun into the waistband of his jeans.

"Is that a gun? What are you doing?"

"Protecting us, I hope," he said. "Let's go."

Outside, he opened the passenger door for her. "Get in."

He eased her door shut and stood, listening. The car engine sound was getting louder every second. They had no time left.

He took one quick look at the shack, hoping they hadn't forgotten anything. Then he went around the car and got in. "You have the phone?"

She nodded.

"Okay." He cranked the car, wincing at the roar of the engine, which he was sure echoed just as loudly through the swamp as the one coming toward them, and rolled the window down.

Paige started to say something, but he held up his hand. He couldn't hear the other engine any longer.

Assessing the condition of the road, he eased forward, concentrating on keeping the car out of the deepest ruts. If he slipped up they would end up stuck in gumbo mud.

The thought of abandoning the car and facing their pursuers or heading out across the swamp on foot was not a pleasant one.

Paige rubbed her eyes and flexed her stiff, sore shoulder gingerly.

"What time is it? Did the cell phone ring?" she asked, digging the phone out of her pocket to look at its face. She breathed a sigh of relief. No missed calls. The digital clock read seven-thirty.

"Why didn't you wake me?" She had wasted precious hours sleeping, hours they could have been looking for Katie.

"You weren't going to do Katie or us any good in the condition you were in with that shoulder. You were on the verge of passing out, anyhow," Johnny said. "Now be quiet so I can hear the other car."

"Other car? What other car?" she asked, tensing, thinking about how urgently he'd woken her and gotten them into the car.

His hands were white-knuckled on the steering wheel. His jaw flexed under a day's growth of stubble and his brow was wrinkled in concentration.

He held up a hand as he listened. "The car that's coming our way."

"Out here?" Paige looked around. "We're in the middle of a swamp. I thought you said nobody knew about this place."

"Nobody does, which means there's probably only one reason another car would be out here." Johnny's eyes flicked downward to the odometer, then back up at the road.

"They've found us."

He nodded, sending her a quick glance. "Yeah."

"What are we going to do?"

"We're going to pray they don't know these roads. Now hold on."

He yanked the steering wheel without slowing down, and the back wheels slid in the mud as he struggled to keep control of the car.

They weren't going fast, but it was obvious how hard Johnny had to work to hold the car in the road and fight the sticky mud that sucked at the tires and plastered itself to the sides and bottom of the car.

Then she saw something through the mist. A dark shape. The other car. It was headed straight for them.

"Johnny, they're coming right at us!"

"No kidding." He cursed, using words and phrases Paige had never heard before. She tensed and braced herself as the black car came closer and closer.

"Hold tight."

"What are you—"

He leaned forward, his teeth clenched in concentration, working the clutch and the gears to keep traction in the mud.

The other car was big and low to the ground. It was caked with mud, and as it came closer, Paige could hear its engine laboring.

It fishtailed once, but its driver compensated and kept coming.

Paige couldn't breathe. She watched in frozen fascination. They were going to crash!

Johnny suddenly went into action, shoving the gearshift into First and yanking the steering wheel to the right. The back wheels spun again, and Paige clung to the armrest as the momentum slung her sideways.

She heard the other engine roar as its driver tried to follow. Then a dull, wet thump echoed through the swamp. Twisting around as much as her sore shoulder would allow, she saw that the other car had missed the road and slammed into a tree. There was no sign of life from inside the vehicle.

"Oh my God, they tried to run us off the road. Do you think they're hurt?"

Johnny took a deep breath and slowed to a stop on a small rise that seemed a bit less muddy. He let the car idle as he flexed his fingers and arched his neck.

"Do you think they're the kidnappers?"

He frowned at her. "I can't figure out who else they'd be. Like I told you before, nobody knows this place."

He pulled the gun from the waistband of his jeans. "I'll go check on them. Maybe get some answers."

"Johnny?"

He stopped with the car door half open.

"Be careful."

Just as he stepped out, a shot rang out and shattered the glass in the driver's side door. He ducked, slipping in the mud.

"Johnny!"

"Get down!" he shouted as a second shot hit metal.

Paige saw him crouching against the car frame, one hand bracing himself, the other holding the gun.

"Get in!" she cried. "Are you hurt?"

"I said get down."

Paige slumped down in the passenger seat just as a bullet hit the rear window.

Johnny climbed back into the car, throwing the mud-spattered gun into her lap, and gunned the engine. For a heart-stopping moment it felt like the car was going to spin down into the mud and leave them trapped.

Finally the back wheels caught and the vehicle lunged forward.

More shots rang out, shrieking as they grazed metal. A couple of them hit the rear window again. Each one stopped Paige's heart for an instant as she waited to see if its impact hit her or Johnny.

But somehow, although bullets continued to ricochet off metal, none hit them as Johnny maneuvered the swamp road with what seemed to Paige like incredible expertise. His entire right side was coated with mud where he'd dropped to the ground when the first shot rang out.

Behind them, a dark figure aimed a gun over the top of the black car as its engine roared helplessly and mud sprayed from under its back wheels.

"Are you all right?" Paige cried.

He nodded as he fought with the car. His broad shoulders bunched with tension and drying mud flecked off his bicep and wrist.

After a few seconds his struggle seemed to ease. The road was changing. It rose a little higher above the surrounding swamp and the surface began to turn to gravel instead of mud.

He relaxed minutely.

Paige couldn't take her eyes off him. He was so focused, so determined, so strong. After that first shocking meeting at the door of his apartment, she hadn't had much of a chance to study the differences in him. She'd been too worried and frightened.

Then the stunning news that Johnny didn't remember her or his life before he was kidnapped had further confused her already muddled brain. She reached out and wiped mud off his cheek. He stiffened, then glanced at her sidelong, his lashes shadowing his eyes.

"We're almost back to the main road," he said curtly. "We've got to decide what to do."

Paige looked in the side mirror. "Do you think they got out of the mud? Do you think they're following us?"

"I think it's real strange that they managed to get as close to us as they did." His voice held an unmistakable note of suspicion.

"What are you saying? You think I somehow led them to us? You think I'd *do* that?"

He pushed mud-encrusted hair off his forehead with an impatient gesture that sent flecks of dried mud flying everywhere.

"Look, Paige. I don't doubt that I knew you in the past. Otherwise you wouldn't be so...in my head." He rubbed his left temple and a grimace of pain crossed his face. "But how do I know what's going on here? How do I know there's a child at all?"

Paige felt the impact of each word as if it were a separate punishing blow. Fury rose inside her like a flame fed by oxygen. He didn't believe her?

Then she thought about what it must have been like for him to hear the things she'd told him. He'd protected her. He'd gotten her safely away from the men who'd attacked them, he'd tenderly cared for her hurt shoulder and he'd watched over her while she slept.

And he'd done it all without knowing anything about who she was.

He only knew one thing for sure, and that was that he'd seen her before. He had no reason to believe what she said, not after she'd brought those men right to his door. How could she convince him she was sincere?

She took in his haggard face, his white-knuckled hands, the bunched tension of his shoulders and gave him the only answer that she thought he could relate to.

"How do I know you really have amnesia?"

His brows shot up and he sent her a look of surprise laced with venom. He started to say something, then clamped his jaw shut.

She pressed her lips together and waited. The next few seconds might decide both their fates.

He looked back at the road then at her again and his mouth turned up just slightly.

"Touché," he muttered.

She relaxed. Their uneasy alliance was still intact. They drove in silence for a while, listening to the car's engine labor under the extra weight of the mud sticking to it. There were loud thumps and metallic clangs as clumps of mud loosened and fell.

Slowly, the landscape began to change, to look more urban. Johnny flexed his hand, cracking dried mud.

"So, Paige. What next? I can't go anywhere looking like this."

She looked behind her and saw the round cracks where bullets had hit the rear window. "I guess we got away from them?"

"For the moment." Johnny frowned. "But how did they find us?"

"Does anybody else know about your cabin? Tante Yvette? The old man on the steps?"

"The old man—you mean Old Mose?" Johnny shook his head. "Old Mose would never..." He stopped and his face reflected a sick horror.

"Johnny?"

"It's Mose's house...his family's house. But he wouldn't—"

Paige closed her eyes. "Maybe he had no choice."

Johnny cursed. "I've got to go to the hotel. I've got to check on him."

"We can't. That's the one place they'd be sure to find us. Please, Johnny. We don't have much time." She touched his muddy arm. "They only gave me until the cell phone battery runs out."

He stared at her. "How long has it been?"

She looked at the face of the phone. "Thirty hours."

He took the next right.

"Where are you taking us?"

"Back to the hotel."

"But, Johnny—"

"They already followed you there. They'd think we'd be fools to go back."

Paige looked at his profile. "Wouldn't we?"

His mouth tightened and his jaw flexed, knocking off a little shower of mud flakes. "I hope not."

JAY PULLED THE CAR into the alley behind the hotel. They were almost out of gas, thanks to the extra load of mud the car was carrying.

He used a few handfuls of the sticky stuff to cover

bullet holes and to finish obscuring the license plate. Standing back, he looked at it critically. Would layers of mud be less noticeable than bullet holes?

The casement window to his apartment was smashed. As they climbed in avoiding the glass, the evidence of struggle was obvious, as was evidence that their pursuers had spent a few minutes searching the room. The mattress and bedclothes were on the floor, and his sketches were torn and scattered.

Except for the drawings, there was nothing here that meant anything to him, but the little room had been the closest thing to home he remembered.

Paige picked up a torn sketch. "Johnny, I'm sorry."

He shrugged. He was, too. Looking at the chaos, he wondered briefly if he'd have been better off never putting the drawing out there. He shook off that notion.

Last night had told him one thing. There might be things in his past that he didn't want to face. Things so awful he couldn't imagine them.

But he was tired of being alone.

He had no memory of anyone depending on him. No purpose that gave meaning to his life. But then Paige had knocked on his door, with her trusting eyes and her desperate plea. She'd given him more in these last few hours than he could remember ever having.

She was the key to his past, and maybe, the doorway to his future.

She stood in the middle of the chaos that had been his room, holding his torn drawings, her expression a mixture of concern and expectation. She was depending on him. God help him—she believed in him.

His reaction was frightening and new. He wanted

to be dependable. He hoped he was the kind of man who could be. He frowned and his skin tightened and itched where the mud had dried. They needed to get going.

"You have the gun, right?" he asked.

She offered it to him, holding it delicately by its handle. He took it and quickly and efficiently cleaned it, using the corner of the sheet from his bed. Then he held it out to her.

"You hang on to this while I clean up."

"I don't—"

Jay put the gun into her small hand and positioned it correctly. "This is the safety. Pushing it this direction makes it possible to fire the gun. Then all you do is pull the trigger."

Her hand tensed under his. "I don't want it," she said.

He tightened his grip reassuringly. "Listen to me, Paige, the window is broken, the door is smashed, and I need to get this mud off me and change clothes. Otherwise, wherever we go I'll be a little conspicuous."

He let go of her hand. "Now, I'll be done in less than two minutes. You put that gun in your pocket. No, put the safety on first. And if you hear anything, you take the safety off, point the gun, and yell for me, okay? You have to do this. It's your life, and your—our daughter's."

She paled, but nodded.

"Good." He let his breath out in a sigh. There was no bathroom, just the door to the toilet on one side of the room and a sink and a shower on the other.

He stood at the sink and started shedding his clothes. When he looked into the mirror, the reflection he saw resembled some bizarre harlequin, with half his body and face covered in mud.

As he peeled off his T-shirt and jeans and dropped his boxers, he was acutely conscious of the woman behind him.

He glanced in the mirror and caught her gaze before she looked away. To his dismay, his body stirred at the thought of her eyes on him.

He clenched his jaw and stepped into the shower.

As good as the hot water felt, he didn't waste any time. Paige was out there alone. He soaped up quickly and rinsed the mud down the drain, then pushed the curtain aside and stepped out, reaching for a towel.

Paige stood like a soldier, stiff and alert, directly opposite the shower. When Jay stepped out, her eyes went wide and she blushed.

"Sorry," he said, grabbing the towel and wrapping it around his middle, trying to ignore the erotic sensation of her eyes on him. "No time or space for modesty."

"Oh, no, that's okay." She sounded choked, but she lifted her gaze to his and for a brief moment something passed between them. Something that felt familiar to Jay.

Something like the memory of love.

Jay searched her face, basking in the idea that she knew him, knew his body. He held on desperately to the sense that he'd seen that look of hunger on her face before.

But she blinked and dropped her gaze, and the sense of déjà vu slipped away.

As he pulled out underwear, jeans and a white button shirt, Paige spoke behind him. "What happened to your hip?"

He tucked in his shirt and buttoned his jeans. Then he pulled on socks and running shoes. That pretty much took care of his wardrobe, he thought wryly.

He grabbed a light windbreaker to hide the gun tucked in his belt.

"I don't know," he said in answer to her question. "The doc at the clinic said it looked like a surgical scar. He offered to x-ray it, but I didn't bother."

He turned to look at her. "Did I not have that scar before?"

Paige had started picking up his sketches, but at his words, she looked up, then straightened. Her cheeks turned pink.

"No." Her eyes flickered downward. "No scar."

She bent down to pick up another drawing.

"Leave those. Let's go."

"No, I want them."

Now that he was cleaned up and dressed, Jay was anxious to check on Old Mose and get away from this place where their pursuers had found him.

"Come on." He led her out through the smashed door and down the hall to the front of the old hotel. He pushed open the front door, and waves of relief washed over him as he saw Old Mose sitting in his usual spot.

"Mose!" he rasped, his throat tight and his eyes burning. Mose had been one of only a few people he'd felt he could trust.

The relief that Old Mose was unharmed was overwhelming.

"Well, well. Jay. I see your pretty vision found you." Mose pulled a greasy paper bag from his pocket and drank from the bottle it hid. "Have some?"

Jay shook his head, smiling at the familiar gesture. Every time he saw Mose, the old man offered him a drink, and every time Jay declined. "Seen anybody suspicious, Mose?"

Mose laughed, then coughed. "I see suspicious every day, son. But if you're talking 'bout those two fellows who ransacked your room, I ain't seen them since they hightailed it outta here all bloody and bruised. Your doing?"

Jay nodded. "You didn't talk to them, did you?"

"Naw. I mostly hid."

Laughter bubbled up inside Jay's chest. He shook his head. "Mose, you are something. Here." He reached into his pocket and pulled out a couple of bills. "Go to the clinic today. They have better medicine than the liquor store does."

"I hear you, son," Mose agreed, nodding as he took the money. "I just might do that. You two on your way then?"

Jay nodded as he put his hand on the small of Paige's back and guided her down the steps. "If anyone comes around asking questions…"

"Old Mose don't know nothing. Old Mose just a drunk." The old man winked at him.

"Thanks, Mose."

Jay glanced around, then ushered Paige around the corner.

"That house in the swamp belongs to Old Mose?"

"Yeah," Johnny said as he guided Paige away from the alley where the car was parked.

"We're not taking the car?"

"Too risky. Those guys might recognize it."

He led them toward a streetcar stop.

"Where are we going?"

"You tell me. I want to see your apartment."

Chapter Five

Paige paused at the door of her apartment, overwhelmed by the remembered horror of finding Katie gone. As she pushed the key into the lock, her eyes lit on a little handprint beside the doorknob.

She reached out and placed her fingers on the smudged outline of her daughter's hand, her heart contracting in worry and grief.

Johnny squeezed her shoulder, but not even the comforting warmth of his hand could quell the dread with which she opened the door. She stepped reluctantly into the living room, her stomach in knots.

The first thing she saw was the phone with its torn, naked wires lying in the middle of the floor. In the neat, orderly room it was the only sign that anything was out of the ordinary.

But nothing would ever be ordinary again. They'd taken her child.

Johnny's hand slid down her arm to clasp her hand.

She stared at the phone for a moment, then walked past it. ''Katie's—'' Her voice echoed in the empty apartment.

A hole had been carved out of her heart when her mother died. Then when Johnny went away it had gaped even larger. But nothing she had ever experienced compared with the empty place inside her now. It seemed bigger than she was.

Without Katie, there would be nothing left of her.

Johnny's fingers tightened reassuringly. "Show me Katie's room."

His calm, clear voice was like a beacon in a dark world. She focused on it, drawing strength from his presence. She had to stay strong for Katie.

She did her best to answer him with the same calmness. "It's in here," she said, stiffening her back as she walked down the hall and entered her daughter's room.

Katie's pink-and-purple comforter was in a heap on the floor where she'd thrown it, and her favorite pillow still had that tiny indentation where her precious head had lain.

"Did you pull the sheets and bedspread off the bed?"

She nodded, her gaze riveted on the pillow. "The cell phone kept ringing and I couldn't find it." Her voice caught.

"It was in here?"

"On her bed. Right there, on the pillow, where…" Paige couldn't make the words come out. She couldn't even get breath. Her child was gone, kidnapped. Held captive God knew where.

The void inside her throbbed.

"I can't stand this," she whispered, her palm pressing on her chest. "I can't do it any more. What if they hurt her?"

"Hey," Johnny said, moving to place his hands gently on her upper arms and rubbing reassuringly.

"Look at me. We will find her. You've done everything they've asked you to do, haven't you?"

She nodded, her eyes dry and burning, her throat aching with unshed tears. "What if it's not enough?"

The cell phone rang.

Paige jumped. She fumbled in her jacket pocket for the phone and the tape recorder. Johnny took the tape recorder from her and pressed the record button. Hands shaking, she answered the phone, holding it at an angle from her ear, near the recorder.

"Katie?" she said, her voice still raspy with emotion.

"Hello, Paige," the disguised voice said. "I have someone who wants to talk to you."

Paige gasped and squeezed the phone so tightly her hands ached.

"Mommy?"

Relief almost buckled her knees to hear that sweet familiar voice.

"Hi, sweetie." Katie never called her Mommy any more. It was Mom or Mother these days. *She must be so scared.*

"Are you okay? Are they feeding you?" She held her breath, expecting to have the phone yanked away from her child any moment, cherishing every breath, every word that kept her connected for one more second to her precious daughter.

"They brought me pizza, but it was cold."

A shaky laugh erupted painfully from Paige's chest. Katie must be okay. She was complaining about cold pizza.

"Are you warm—"

"Mommy, do you know where my daddy is?"

Paige's heart slammed into her chest wall. "Katie,

honey, what do you mean? What have they told you, sweetie?''

''Mommy, please. I don't like it here. Come and get—''

Her scared little voice stopped abruptly.

''Katie!''

''Hello, Paige. It's so hard to control emotional little girls, isn't it?''

''I swear to you if you hurt one hair on my child's head, I'll—''

''You'll what?'' Laughter crackled like static in her ear. Paige wished she could tell if it was a man or a woman. ''You're not in a position to make threats. You're running out of time. Your phone's battery is probably half run-down already.''

''Where do you want me to go? Give me a time. Give me a place and I'll be there. You're the one delaying.''

''All the better to see you squirm, Paige.'' The voice went brittle with anger. ''You are under my control and you will do as I say. Make no mistake about it. You so much as nod at a policeman, and you will never see your child again.''

''I've given you my word. I won't tell anyone. Just tell me where to be and when. I'll be there.''

The phone went dead.

Paige stared at the quiet phone, then raised her gaze to Johnny's. He was watching her, his face grave, his brow wrinkled in concern.

''She called me *Mommy*. She never does that anymore. She's so scared.''

Johnny's eyes glinted with sadness. ''I know. We'll find her. I promise.''

He brushed the corner of her lip with his thumb,

then wrapped his hand around her nape and pressed a kiss to her forehead. His warm fingers, his gentle kiss, made her want to believe in his promise.

She met his gaze and saw in it a reflection of the boy she had known, and remembered his earnest vow that he would never leave her.

She'd believed his promises before.

She pulled away from his touch, anger burning through her grief. "Don't patronize me. You can't promise me we'll find her. You can't promise me anything."

She made a sound somewhere between a laugh and a sob. "You don't even remember who you are!"

He grasped her arms. "Paige, calm down. If we're going to stand a chance of finding her, we've got to work together."

She jerked against his grip again, but he held firm, the determination in his face reminding her that he was no longer the boy who had left her.

Everything about him exuded strength and dependability. His strength called to her, as did his calm words.

He was right. She had to believe in him. She had no other choice.

She nodded, picking up Katie's pillow, hugging it to her, breathing in the faint scent of bubblegum shampoo.

Johnny looked at the tape recorder in his hand.

He rewound the tape, then listened. Paige sat stiffly as her pleading and Katie's scared little voice reverberated in the room.

When the caller's voice came on, Johnny's grip tightened on the recorder and he frowned. He stopped the tape, then played it back again, louder. Then he turned the volume down and held it close to his ear, his eyes closed.

His face drained of color, his lips were compressed into a thin line.

"Listen to this," he said, rewinding it again. "Can you tell what those sounds in the background are?"

He hit Play.

Paige listened, shaking her head. "There's a creaking noise, and something else."

"A train," he said, his voice strained.

She looked up at him. "A train?" Her heart leapt in hope. "Do you know where they are?"

He shook his head, a bewildered frown marring his features. "I'm not sure."

"You're not sure? Then what do we do? We can't just wait around for them to call."

Johnny wiped his face and directed his full attention back to her. "We won't. I want you to talk me through the evening Katie was kidnapped. I need to understand everything that happened. You went to a party. When did you get there? What time did you leave? Did anything odd happen?"

His steady, even tone, and his logical words buoyed her spirits a bit. Still holding on to Katie's pillow, she told him about the charity benefit, describing everything she could remember about the evening.

"It was one of Sally's classic events. An art auction to benefit a home for pregnant teens."

"And when you left here everything was fine?"

Paige's breath caught. She nodded. "Katie wasn't happy with me for going. It was pizza night. And she was supposed to start her second year of swimming lessons the next day."

"How long did you stay?"

Johnny was moving around the room, his keen gaze roaming over every square inch. He picked up a pink stuffed bear off the floor, holding it for a brief moment before setting it on the bed.

She grabbed the bear. "Too long. I was about to leave around eleven-thirty, when Sally found me and pulled me into one of her famous little dramas. She unveiled your drawing to me in front of all the guests."

Johnny studied the bookcase where Katie's favorite books and videos were stacked. He picked up the Mardi Gras mask Katie had made herself from papiér-mâché and painted in garish yellow and red and chartreuse. He moved to the open closet door, his hand sliding across Katie's clothes.

Watching him touch her daughter's things sent conflicting feelings through Paige. A part of her wanted to push his hand away from her child's clothes. But she couldn't ignore the look of longing on his face and the tenderness with which his fingers paused on Katie's blue denim jumper.

They were *his* daughter's things too.

"What are you looking for?"

His head angled toward her, but his eyes lingered for a moment on the little dress.

"Anything that might give us a clue." He faced her. "What's missing?"

A numbing shock froze her. "I didn't think about that. I should have checked." She went over to the closet, running her hands across the hangers. Katie's clothes were so tiny.

"She's so little, so helpless." She reluctantly let go of Katie's favorite Sunday dress, a red plaid one with a little black bow at the neck.

"When I left she had on jeans and a New Orleans Saints T-shirt," she said, thinking back to earlier that evening, as she was getting ready to go out. Her memory of it was bright and clear and happy. Everything since seemed dull and colorless.

She picked up the sheets and shook them, then tossed them onto the bed. "She usually leaves her clothes on the floor or on top of the cedar chest." She pointed to the chest at the end of Katie's bed.

"They're gone." She picked up the bedspread, then looked around. "So are her tennis shoes. And of course Ugly Afghan." She suppressed a horrific vision of big faceless men wrapping her child in the afghan and carrying her away.

Johnny bent down and picked up something off the floor. He handed it to her.

"Her sock." Paige squeezed the little sock in her fist and sat back down on the edge of the bed. "She only has one sock. She's so particular about her socks. They have to be just right. No wrinkles, no twists."

She felt like she was about to come undone. "Do you think they'll buy her some socks? They won't, will they?"

She looked up at Johnny, and caught an odd expression on his face.

"She has her afghan," he said softly.

Paige nodded, holding on to control with every bit of strength she had. "She named it Ugly Afghan. It's orange and green. She loves to wrap up in it." She swallowed against the lump that kept growing in her throat and took a deep breath. She wiped her face and pushed at stray tendrils of hair.

"You were telling me about Sally showing you the

drawing,'' Johnny said quietly. "What happened after that?''

She forced her brain to focus on the party, rather than on Katie. She closed her eyes, reliving the instant when she'd first seen the picture.

"Everything faded into the background except the picture. I felt like I was going to faint when I saw your signature and the date. I thought you were dead.''

He glanced over at her, his mouth twisted wryly. "Apparently somebody else did too, until something happened to let them know I wasn't. Tante Yvette told me a redhead in a man's hat and jacket bought the drawing.''

Paige had to smile. "That's Sally. She's always roaming around little dusty shops looking for new artists.''

"Who all was at the party?''

She shook her head. "I don't know those people. We could probably get a guest list from Sally.''

"If you didn't know anyone, then what was she doing parading you and the drawing in front of them?''

"You'd have to know Sally. This was a benefit. The guests were there to buy art. The whole evening was about unveiling the drawing and presenting me right there beside it. It creates excitement and people tend to spend more.''

Johnny looked thoughtful. "How do you know someone didn't put her up to it?''

"No one puts Sally up to anything.''

"But for all you know she could be involved.''

"Involved in kidnapping Katie?'' Paige was shocked. "No! Sally loves Katie.''

"Did she say anything?" He walked over to the window, examined the casement and peered out through the curtains.

Paige shook her head. "We didn't talk much. She mentioned the idea of having a showing of children's art so Katie could come with me next time."

"You talked about Katie? Did anyone overhear you?"

A sick dread enveloped Paige. She closed her eyes, trying to remember if anyone had been standing close to them.

"There were a lot of people there. It was crowded." Paige stood, too agitated and worried to sit any longer. "I suppose anyone could have heard us."

"Did anyone remark about the resemblance between you and the drawing?"

"Yes, almost everybody did."

"Okay. Who *didn't* say anything to you?" He picked up the comforter and shook it carefully.

"I told you, I only knew a very few people there. There were several who didn't say anything. The woman in the Dalmatian wrap for one."

He stopped, the multicolored material draped over his hands. "Dalmatian?"

Paige smiled. "She had black hair with a white streak, and she looked just like a cartoon villainess."

He stared at her.

She laughed shakily. "There was a Penguin who didn't speak to me either. A little round man with a monocle."

Talking about the characters she'd seen made her remember how excited she'd been about sharing them with Katie.

"Katie would have loved to see them. *101 Dalmatians* is her favorite movie."

Suddenly, the grief and fear were too much. They washed over her in punishing waves. She hiccoughed, then gasped. She felt as if she was suffocating. Her chest heaved as she sucked in air in gulping sobs, but it didn't help. She covered her mouth with her hands, trying to stop her out-of-control breathing.

A strong, sheltering warmth enveloped her as Johnny pulled her into his embrace and pressed her face into the hollow of his shoulder.

She huddled there, surrounded by his strength. Her labored breathing slowed as she inhaled his warm, faintly soapy scent.

Comforted by his solid bulk, her body relaxed, molding naturally against his, drawing hope from his presence. "Oh, Johnny, I missed you so."

JAY HAD INTENDED TO comfort Paige and stop her from hyperventilating, but as her frantic breaths calmed, she moved closer to him.

Too close for comfort.

He felt his body reacting and gritted his teeth. It had been a long time since he'd held a woman. He didn't like impersonal coupling for a few minutes relief, and it wasn't easy to connect with someone else when you didn't know who you were.

But this small woman seemed to fit perfectly with him, not only physically, but in other, less easily explained ways. His brain didn't remember her, but his body recognized the shape, the feel, of hers.

It was pure torture, holding her like this, trying to comfort her when he could barely control his male response to her supple skin and her smooth, silky hair.

He felt her pulling away. He let her.

Clamping his jaw, keeping control of his baser instincts by sheer force of will, he stepped backward, placing his hands on her shoulders, holding her at arm's length.

If he was going to be able to find her daughter—their daughter—he needed to focus.

He was convinced that someone at that party other than Paige had been surprised to see his drawing and discover that he wasn't dead. He had to figure out who that person was, and how they'd managed to formulate a kidnapping plan so quickly.

Paige's face was pale, her eyes haunted, but she'd stopped gasping for each breath. As he watched, she straightened and seemed to gather determination from somewhere inside herself.

She was strong. She had to be, to have borne and raised a child alone, to have made this life for herself and her child.

Jay felt a measure of anger and disgust for the boy he had been. He'd give anything to know why he'd left her, but at the same time, the answer scared him to death. Surely he'd loved and admired her strength as much then as he did now.

She brushed strands of blond hair from her face and blinked. "I kept trying to leave the party, but I couldn't get away for over an hour. Everybody was talking to me, asking me about the drawing. I finally worked my way over to the door and slipped out. I took a cab home and found Dawn sitting outside in her boyfriend's car."

"Dawn is your baby-sitter?"

"Not my regular sitter. She was new."

"Did you talk to her?"

"No. I was furious. I told her you never leave a child alone—"

Her voice broke as another little sob escaped. "I sent her home and told her I'd be talking to her mother."

"Could she have been in on it?" He doubted it, but he needed Paige to consider every possibility.

Paige frowned. "I don't think so. She's only fifteen. My regular sitter couldn't make it and she suggested her friend Dawn. Sally's invitation was last-minute."

"It wouldn't hurt to talk to her. She might have seen something."

A look of wary hope crossed her face. "Maybe she did! I've got her telephone number somewhere."

"Good. We'll talk to her as soon as we're through here."

He stepped out into the hall. "Is that your bedroom?"

When he entered the other bedroom the first thing he noticed was Paige's bed. Neat, untouched, it was a symbol of her ordeal. It hadn't been slept in.

The bedroom phone lay on the floor, its wires ripped from the wall just like the one in the living room.

As he checked the windows and the carpet, looking for a footprint, a mark, anything that might yield a clue about the kidnappers, his gaze fell on a small, framed picture on Paige's nightstand.

His heart turned upside down in his chest. He could hardly catch a breath. A throbbing ache began in his temple.

He stepped closer, unable to take his eyes off the photo.

A little girl with long blond hair and his own startling blue eyes gazed back at him. She was grinning, revealing a missing tooth.

"This is Katie." His voice cracked on her name. This was his daughter. A daughter he hadn't known he had. Conceived in a time he didn't remember with a woman whose face was only familiar to him as a bright vision amongst nightmares.

He picked up the picture with unsteady hands. "She's beautiful," he whispered. "Just like you."

His fingers tightened reflexively. He had a child.

Those four words were like a sunrise, pulling his world out of darkness.

A child. A connection to his past. A thread that stretched through the lonely world he'd inhabited for three years.

His eyes misted over. After all this time, he was no longer alone and nameless. This child was proof of that.

But something about him, something in his past had placed his beautiful, innocent daughter in danger. Tightening his grip on the picture, Jay silently vowed to save his child or die trying.

He looked at Paige, whose gaze was glued to the picture. She took it from his hands.

The gesture hurt him, deep inside. She hadn't said a word, hadn't even looked at him, but her condemnation was loud and clear.

He didn't have a right to Katie's picture. He wasn't to be trusted any more than absolutely necessary for Paige to find her daughter.

She would trade him for Katie if she had to.

"Paige?"

She lifted her chin determinedly. When her gaze met his, her eyes were dark with sadness and fear.

"I don't remember you, except as a dream. I don't know why any of this has happened. But I do know Katie is my daughter. I will not let anyone hurt her, I swear to you."

Paige's eyes widened, filled with a look he couldn't read.

"I'll offer myself for her."

She looked down at the picture, touching the glass, then back up at him. Something changed in her eyes. A hint of wary trust replaced a bit of the desolation there.

He wasn't sure if he was worthy of that trust, but he knew, for his daughter's sake, that he would die rather than betray it.

"I hope it doesn't come to that," she whispered.

THEY SAT IN THE LIVING room of Dawn's parents' house, waiting for Dawn's boyfriend to get there.

Dawn looked pale and nervous, fiddling with her short black hair and playing with the belt buckle on her low-rise jeans.

When her boyfriend arrived and sat beside Dawn, his hair longer than hers and his Tulane University T-shirt hanging loosely over his baggy pants, Paige asked them what they'd seen that night.

"Katie's okay, isn't she, Ms. Reynolds? I mean, I was only outside for a minute."

Paige tried to speak, but her throat closed up. Desperate, hurting, wanting to lash out at this irresponsible teen who had left her child alone, she met Johnny's gaze, pleading silently with him to help her.

"Everything's fine, Dawn," he said curtly. "It's

just that the back door was open and something is missing."

Paige bit her lip to keep from crying out in pain at his words. *Something.*

"We didn't take anything, honest," Dawn said.

"Hey, wait a minute." Her boyfriend sat up from his slouched position on the couch. "I never even went inside."

"We're not accusing you. Either of you. We just need to know if you noticed anything."

"Nah," the boyfriend said.

"Like what?" Dawn asked at the same time.

Paige swallowed hard, doing her best to keep her emotions in check. Dawn was watching her with a fearful expression, and Paige knew her grief and panic must be clearly visible.

Johnny stood, towering over the two teens. "Anything at all. Was there a sound, a strange vehicle, somebody running?" He leaned just slightly toward the boyfriend and looked him in the eye. "This is very important, if you get my meaning. Did I understand Ms. Reynolds to say that Dawn is just fifteen? So you're what? Eighteen?"

The boyfriend looked at him guiltily. "Whoa, man. We weren't doing nothing. Just talking."

"Then you don't have a problem. Now think."

Paige heard the menace in Johnny's voice. These glimpses of his new hardness, his increased physical strength, sometimes took her by surprise. A tiny flame of hope flared inside her. This man was capable of things the boy she'd known could never have done.

"There was this one thing."

Paige's attention jerked back to the boyfriend. "What?" she cried.

Johnny's hand touched her arm, sending her a reassuring signal.

"Yeah?" he said. "What one thing?"

"Well, man, right after she—Ms. Reynolds—went inside her apartment, this van comes from out of nowhere. It squealed out from behind us and almost hit my car."

Paige's hands gripped each other tightly. "Oh my God! I was there." Had Katie been in that van?

"What kind of van?" Johnny stood over the two, looking at them with a menacing frown.

Dawn shrank back into the couch.

Her boyfriend swallowed audibly, then spoke. "White. Dirty. Old."

"It just had one taillight," Dawn said. "I remember." She turned to her boyfriend. "You cursed at it."

"And this was right after Ms. Reynolds got home?"

The boyfriend nodded. "The cab almost hit it pulling away from the curb."

Johnny held out his hand to Paige. "Okay," he said to the kids. "Thanks."

As Johnny took Paige's arm and guided her toward the door, Dawn spoke.

"Ms. Reynolds, I'm really sorry. I'm glad Katie is all right."

Paige turned back to look at her. Johnny's hand on her arm gave her the strength to walk out of the house.

Paige put her hands over her mouth and took slow, calm breaths. "She's glad Katie is all right," she gasped, almost laughing. "She's glad—"

Johnny's gentle hands guided her toward the streetcar stop. "It's probably a good thing Dawn chose that moment to go outside," he said.

At his words, Paige stopped in her tracks. "What are you talking about? She let Katie be kidnapped. She left my child alone!"

Johnny turned to face her. "If she had been inside, they might have killed her."

Chapter Six

"I am sick of your excuses," Serena said, lighting another cigarette with the crystal lighter on her desk. "Why do I keep you on my payroll?"

"Watch it, sis. You need me, and I'm cheap at the price."

"I'm beginning to think I don't need you at all Leonard. Now what is the problem this time?"

"Maybe you don't understand how GPS works, but—"

"I understand exactly how global positioning satellite systems work, you nitwit. What you obviously don't understand is that when I said minute by minute surveillance, that's precisely what I meant."

Serena blew smoke out in agitated puffs as she paced in front of the glass wall of her executive suite on the top floor of the Yarbrough Industries Corporate Offices.

She was tired of her brother and his incompetent hirelings, tired of waiting, tired of having to be sure Johnny's brat was taken care of.

"I've got a man watching the screen twenty-four-seven."

"Then how did you lose them?" Serena said through clenched teeth. "Never mind. Just remember that you don't get anything until the targets are taken care of. I hope I don't have to end up handling this. Do I make myself clear?"

"Oh, you're clear, Sue Ann."

"Never call me that. You have twenty-four hours. She's beginning to ask why I haven't set up a meeting place."

"And you don't care how it's done?"

Serena felt like screaming. "Of course I don't care how it's done. Now quit bothering me. If you can't get a fix on them, they're obviously inside a building or the phone is shielded by metal. Send your men back to her apartment to wait until the signal pops up again."

"What a great idea," her brother said sarcastically.

"Just make sure they don't forget to retrieve that damn cell phone. I want nothing pointing back to me. Is that clear?"

"Oh, clear as a bell, sis. Are you going to see the little brat today?"

"Is Martin watching her?"

"Yeah. That old softy's probably brought her more movies."

"Then no. I trust Martin. He won't let anything happen to her."

She disconnected and slammed the phone down. Leonard had better hope his goons didn't botch the job this time, or he might find out he'd lost his meal ticket.

Crushing her cigarette out, Serena sighed. It was so hard to get good help these days.

"WHERE ARE WE GOING NOW?" Paige asked as they left her apartment.

"To the library. I need to dig up everything we can find on the Yarbroughs."

Paige nodded. She knew he had so many questions about the life he couldn't remember. Yet, ever since he'd opened his apartment door to her, he'd spent his time helping her. *Helping his daughter.* "What time is it?"

"Around six o'clock. I think."

Paige considered. "All the public libraries are closed by now. If we take the Riverfront streetcar downtown, we can switch to the St. Charles Line. That'll take us to the Monroe Library at Loyola University. I think it's open late."

They climbed onto the streetcar and she leaned wearily against the hard seat back.

Johnny sat stiffly, his sharp eyes assessing the other passengers, scanning the street signs, alert to anything unusual.

She took the opportunity to study his face. "Katie looks so much like you."

He glanced at her in surprise. Then his expression softened as his gaze searched her face. "In the picture in your room she looked like you."

"Look at this." Paige dug her wallet out of her jeans and pulled out a school picture. It was wrinkled. She smoothed it out, her fingers lingering on Katie's precious face, then handed it to Johnny.

"It's this year's. See those blue eyes, and the way she cocks that eyebrow?"

Her vision grew blurry and she had to blink to see.

Johnny held the little square of paper gingerly, as if he were afraid he'd damage it.

"What grade is she in?" he asked without looking up. His voice was hushed.

"She just got out of first grade. She's so smart."

He ran his thumb across the little face. "She looks happy."

The lump in Paige's throat almost choked her. "She is."

"What about—I mean..." Johnny paused and glanced sideways at Paige. "Has she ever had a father?"

Paige looked at the only man she'd ever loved and shook her head. She had to swallow before she could speak. "No. It's always been just Katie and me."

"What about your parents?"

"My parents?" The word called up old regret and grief. "It was always just my mom. My father was married. He disappeared when Mom got pregnant with me."

"That must have been tough for you."

Paige uttered an ironic little laugh. "Hey, he wouldn't have been much of a father if he didn't even care enough to stick around."

Johnny glanced at her sharply, and she realized what she'd said. She opened her mouth to apologize, to tell him she wasn't deliberately drawing a parallel between him and her absent father.

The parallel was there. She just hoped she had not become just like her mother, spending her life mourning a man who had walked away and left her without a word.

The streetcar clattered to a halt at a car stop and Paige realized Johnny was still staring at Katie's picture.

As the car started up again, he spoke. "She must be a handful. She has your stubborn chin."

Paige watched his gaze devouring every detail of the photo. Finally he held it out to her.

"Johnny?"

He lifted his gaze to meet hers. She touched his hand.

"You can keep it."

He blinked. "Are you sure?"

The yearning in his voice almost made Paige cry. She swallowed hard and smiled. "I'm sure."

He looked at the picture again, then tucked it carefully into his shirt pocket, his hand lingering there over his heart for an instant.

"We should get off here," she said, noticing that they were coming to the Canal streetcar stop. "Then we can walk up Canal to Carondolet and catch the St. Charles car."

As they climbed off the streetcar and walked away from the river, Paige felt an overwhelming exhaustion and despair.

Johnny seemed to sense it, because he put his arm around her shoulders for a brief squeeze. Her throat closed. What would she have done without him? He'd kept her safe, kept her focused.

The shadows were growing longer as they approached the end of Canal Street, and a slight breeze lifted strands of her hair.

Johnny put his hand on the small of her back. Unlike his earlier, comforting squeeze, this touch was hard with tension. "Slow down," he said softly.

"What is it?" Her heart sped up at the warning in his tone. Her knees wobbled, but she managed to keep from stumbling.

"Look at that van that just pulled over in front of us. Do you see it?"

Paige slowed her pace, matching it to Johnny's. She looked at the vehicle several yards in front of them that seemed to be keeping pace. It was white. Dirty. Old.

And one taillight was out. Paige's heart pounded and her skin tightened. It was them.

Johnny's hand slid down to take hers. He lifted it to his lips. "Just walk calmly," he said, his breath warm on her skin. "It could be nothing."

"It's not nothing," she said without taking her eyes off the van. Dark shapes moved inside it. Cars honked, trying to get around it.

"I know." His voice was harsh.

"What do we do?"

"Keep walking. Where does this cross street go?"

Paige tore her eyes away from the van. "This is Tchoupotoulas. We can head out toward Loyola."

"Okay, when I stop, you turn to me and give me your other hand, then we'll walk up that street, okay?"

Paige swallowed. "Okay."

They stopped. Johnny met her eyes and nodded, then they turned and started walking on Tchoupotoulas.

The normal street sounds of the early evening were split by a screech of brakes and a grinding of gears as the van stopped, then reversed, backing toward them. It slammed into a car and spun halfway around in the street.

Horns blared and people shouted as the van bullied its way across three lanes of traffic.

"Run!" Johnny shouted.

Paige ran.

Johnny caught her hand and pulled her along until she felt like her feet barely touched the ground. Her sore shoulder cramped with pain.

Behind her she heard the commotion created by the white van. Then suddenly the air was split by the wailing of a police siren.

Her heart leapt into her throat as Johnny urged her faster and faster.

Her breath whistled in her ears as she ran, leaving the commotion farther and farther behind them.

She heard more screeches, and metal crunching, then the sound of an engine gaining on them.

Johnny slowed down a bit, glancing back.

Something flew past her ear.

"Paige!"

He let go of her hand and wrapped his arm around her waist. He practically threw her into an alley between two sets of buildings, an alley too small for the van.

"Are you all right?" he puffed as he pulled her past piles of garbage, boxes, gas cans and broken beach chairs.

She nodded, just as their feet got tangled in a snarl of fence wire and they almost fell. A sharp piece of wire scraped her arm.

Johnny regained his footing before she did. He picked her up and urged her forward. She clung to his arm, running with him, her chest burning as she gasped for breath in the cloying stench of the alley. They dodged cardboard containers and garbage bags.

She looked behind them and saw two figures stop at the entrance to the alley. One of them shouted and pointed.

"They're—right behind us!" she panted.

A shot ricocheted off a building.

"Johnny!" she gasped, shock stealing what little breath she had left. "That was a gunshot!"

They were *shooting* at them!

Johnny grabbed her up and they hurtled down the alley. A break in the buildings opened up and he paused for a heart-stopping second, then pushed her ahead of him.

"What are you doing?" she cried.

"Run!"

He pulled the gun from under his jacket.

Paige felt like she was watching a video in slow motion. Time seemed to stretch out forever as Johnny whirled, wrapping his long artist's fingers around the grip of the deadly weapon. He leaned one shoulder against the corner of the building, then leaned out, his left arm still braced against the building.

Then her vision returned to normal speed as he quickly fired off two shots, then two more.

Paige heard a yelp.

"Be careful," she gasped.

Johnny whipped around and pushed her. "I told you to run!"

She overbalanced but caught herself. Her tennis shoes slapped on the hot asphalt as she ran.

Behind her, she heard Johnny's longer strides. They made it to the street and crossed it, then ducked behind another set of buildings.

Johnny stopped, leaning against the building, trying to catch his breath. Paige's chest hurt. She'd long since forgotten how to breathe. She heaved, desperate for oxygen.

"You—hit—one?"

Johnny nodded, wiping his face on his sleeve. "I think so. But we've got to get out of here."

Paige looked around.

"Do you know where we are?"

She shook her head, still gasping for breath. "There's a big—street over there. If we could—find a streetcar—"

He nodded and took her hand. "Let's go."

But as they changed direction, their pursuers appeared at the edge of the buildings behind them down the alley. The bigger man lifted his gun and shot.

Someone inside one of the apartments screamed, and the squeal of sirens echoed in Paige's ears.

"Police!"

Johnny nodded. "I know. We've got to get out of here."

Johnny hugged the side of the building, putting his body between her and the men. Another shot ricocheted off brick with a screech.

Paige's muscles cramped as she cringed, waiting for a bullet to tear into her flesh, or Johnny's.

They flung themselves around another corner and suddenly they were out in the open, on a busy street. A streetcar stop was only a few yards away, across the street. A crowd of people stood around waiting, probably headed home after work.

Johnny's hand was hot and strong on her back as they walked quickly over and insinuated themselves into the middle of the crowd. Paige tried to breathe normally, praying they weren't putting these innocent people in danger by standing in their midst.

She and Johnny both watched the street, expecting any second to see the white van coming at them, or the two men barreling toward them, but although the street was filled with traffic, the dirty white van didn't show up.

A police car with lights flashing and sirens wailing stopped at the alley where their pursuers had been. Two policemen got out, pistols drawn, and walked between the buildings.

Paige winced and wished she and Johnny could turn invisible. She waited for the sound of gunfire, but then the streetcar came, its clatter drowning out all other sound.

When they finally got onto the car, still out of breath, they had to stand because of the crowd.

Johnny grabbed on to a pole and Paige held on to his arm. His chest still labored. Her own heart was beating frantically.

"Do you know where we are?" Johnny whispered.

Paige looked around, trying to identify a street or an intersection.

A little old woman dressed in a shapeless house-dress and clutching a shopping bag smiled at her. "This is the St. Charles line, honey. You're headed out toward Carrollton. The French Quarter is the other way."

"Is that good?" Johnny muttered.

Paige nodded against his chest. "We're going toward Loyola."

She felt him relax slightly. As the streetcar bumped along, she wrapped her arms around his waist under his windbreaker. Her hands encountered the still-warm gun. She avoided touching it.

"Johnny? Those men were shooting at us. Do you think they were trying to kill us? Or just frighten us?"

He looked down at her, his blue eyes steely and hard.

"But that means—" She couldn't finish the thought.

"They have no intention of giving Katie back. They want us dead."

JAY WATCHED PAIGE RUB her neck as she stared at the computer screen. She was so tired she could hardly keep her eyes open, yet she hadn't complained once.

His hand that held a cup of water shook slightly. He was still spooked by their latest encounter with the goons chasing them. He couldn't believe he'd actually hit one of them. He'd never even shot the gun before.

"How's it going?" he asked Paige, looking over her shoulder.

She let out a frustrated sigh. "There are dozens of references to the Yarbroughs," she said. "Your family has always been very prominent. This is going to take all night."

"Drink this," Jay said, handing her the cup of water.

She took it and drank gratefully.

Sitting down at the computer workstation next to her, he asked, "What are we looking at?"

She slid a CD into his computer. "I'm searching for any articles about your family. This one is dated around the time you graduated from Harvard."

"I went to Harvard?"

She sent him a tired smile and manipulated his mouse until a screen came up. Then she rubbed her eyes.

"Are you okay?"

She nodded and raised her tired gaze to his. "I'm

fine. You search those articles and I'll work with another CD.''

She turned back to the stack of CDs beside her computer and selected another one.

For a moment, Jay just watched her. She looked small and innocent in the big wooden library chair, her hair falling out of its restraining braid. A strand of hair tickled her cheek and she pushed it away. It fell back, and he resisted the urge to reach out and smooth it for her.

He thought about the men chasing them, and the gunshots that had come so close to her. He'd only known her for two days, and already he knew that he would give his life to protect her.

As if she felt him watching her, she turned her head and met his gaze, her face pinched and worried. ''Do you think they'd kill her?''

He wished he could give her a guarantee. But all he could offer was what he thought was true. ''I don't think they'd hurt a child. They're after me, remember? And they probably think I know who they are. They don't know I have amnesia.''

Her gaze sharpened. ''No, you're right. They don't.'' With a tiny smile, she turned back to the computer screen.

He scanned the archives room of the library. He'd chosen the last two workstations so they could have a clear view of the entire floor.

In front of them on the other side of the long room were the elevators, and directly beside them were the stairs. If anyone approached either way, he would know.

He turned to the computer, and entered the word Yarbrough in the search function.

One of the references that came up was subtitled "Son Follows in Father's Footsteps."

He stared at the screen. The article was a feature about shipping magnate Madison Yarbrough and his son, John Andrew Yarbrough. Jay studied the picture that accompanied the article. A solemn young man stood next to a distinguished-looking older man. The two looked remarkably alike.

Jay studied the faces. Was that younger face his? If pressed, he'd admit the face looked familiar. But deep within him, where hope wouldn't die, he couldn't find a real memory of either of the men. Was that straight, tall, confident businessman his father?

Leaning close, he studied the older man dispassionately. He had no feeling of connection with the man in the picture, but it was grainy and faded.

A look in his eyes and his grip on the younger man's shoulder made Jay uncomfortable for some reason. Somehow, the weight of that hand felt heavy on his own shoulder. He shrugged, trying to rid himself of the feeling.

It was hard to imagine himself as a businessman. Easier to envision a young man who wanted to be an artist, but was pressured by his father to enter the family business. But then how would he know?

He checked the date of the article. January, over a year after he'd left Paige alone. Alone and pregnant, just like her father had left her mother.

His gaze went back to the younger man's face. Was he John Andrew Yarbrough? He didn't want to be, if that meant he'd left Paige alone and gone back to his wealthy, privileged life.

Irritated, he hit the print function.

An hour or so later he had found several more articles, most of them having to do with his kidnapping. He printed them out and stacked them up, then sat down and rubbed his eyes.

He picked up the top article and began to read, hope and dread warring inside him. Contained in these pages was the past he'd been seeking.

He was about to learn who he had been.

PAIGE OPENED HER EYES and squinted at the sunlight pouring in an unfamiliar window. She realized she was sitting at a computer workstation with her chin propped on her hand.

Awareness came rushing over her like a tidal wave. Katie was out there locked up in the dark, and she had fallen asleep.

"Johnny, it's morning," she cried, shaking her numb hand. The feeling rushed back into her fingers, prickling them like pins and needles.

He looked up, bleary-eyed.

"We fell asleep!"

He squinted at the clock over the elevator, then stretched and groaned. "Only a few hours. I told you the security guards would believe we were with the group of students studying for exams all night."

Paige groaned as her stiff muscles protested. "Only a few hours? That's great. What about Katie?" She felt frantically in her jacket, her hand closing around the cell phone. "Did they call? Did the phone ring?"

Johnny shook his head. "No. Nobody called. I gathered up the printouts. Take a look at this."

He held out the stack of paper.

Glaring at him, she took it.

Son Follows in Father's Footsteps.

Her breath caught. There it was, picture and all.

The first time she'd ever known who Johnny really was.

It stunned her just like it had the first time she'd seen it. Heartbreak and the empty horror of abandonment rushed through her again, ringing with the awful truth.

He had never loved her. He'd never meant to come back for her. How had she let herself forget that?

She had come so close to trusting him when she'd watched him look at Katie's picture in her bedroom. The combination of awe, yearning and joy that had lit his sharp features as he gazed upon the image of his daughter for the first time had surprised her, as had her own reaction.

It had hurt, seeing him looking at Katie like that. Hurt in a primal, inexplicable way, as if he were stealing some of her daughter from her. That was why she'd taken the picture out of his hands.

But then he'd made his amazing offer to trade himself for their child. A totally unselfish offer that had melted her heart with its sincerity.

She pressed her lips together. That was a different man than the one who had left her. When he remembered who he really was, he would also remember that he hadn't cared enough to come back for her.

She stared at the newspaper article that had dashed her naive hopes, and felt betrayed all over again. As much as she hated to admit it, her mother's bitter words rang true. They echoed down the corridors of Paige's memory.

You can't trust a man, Paige, honey. It's just in their nature. Just look what your daddy did to me.

She'd heard it all her life. As soon as her father

had found out she was on the way, he'd walked out, back to his wife and the children he really wanted.

Paige thrust the printouts back at Johnny, but he pointed to Madison Yarbrough. "Is that really my father?"

The wistful hope in his voice scored another gash into her bleeding heart. "Johnny, he's dead. I'm sorry. He died a couple of years ago, after you disappeared."

He held her gaze for a second, then looked down.

Hurting for him, Paige shuffled the pages, looking at the other articles he'd found. There were several references to the kidnapping, the articles varying from front-page news to small snippets as information dwindled and hope died.

The last big article, featuring Madison Yarbrough in a final hopeless interview, begging for his son's life, included a picture of the businessman and his second wife and her infant son.

Paige looked more closely at the image. There was something familiar about the woman.

"Johnny!" Paige whispered loudly. "Look at this!"

He leaned over her shoulder.

"See that woman? That's her."

"Who?" Johnny leaned closer, until Paige could smell the combination of clean skin, soap and maleness that she was coming to associate with him. She held her breath and focused on the picture.

"Remember?" she asked. "The woman I told you about, at Sally's party. The one with the white streak in her hair. I think she's Serena Yarbrough!"

"She's not my mother?"

Paige heard the strain and guarded hope in his

voice. *Oh, Johnny.* How much disappointment could
he take? She shook her head. "Your stepmother.
Your mother died when you were young. You gave
me this ring that had belonged to her."

He took her outstretched hand in his, touching the
sapphires that shaped the Yarbrough logo. He spoke
without looking up. "I don't remember them. It
shouldn't bother me to find out they're dead."

He didn't speak for a moment. "But somehow it
does."

Paige wanted to wrap her arms around him and
hold him. She wanted to give him reassurance, and
absorb his strength. But even though he held her
hand, there was something remote about him. He
seemed distracted.

His thumb caressed her ring. "You've worn my
ring all this time?"

She pulled away, not wanting to talk about why
she'd kept the ring. Why she'd never taken it off her
engagement finger.

"If that was your stepmother at the party, and she
saw the drawing, she must have realized it was
yours."

He retrieved the printout and studied the picture.
"You didn't recognize her at the party?"

Page shook her head. "This picture was taken after
you were kidnapped. She didn't have that white streak
in her hair back then, and she must have lost at least
thirty pounds since then."

"Do you think she kidnapped Katie?"

Paige thought about the woman's hostile gaze and
shivered. "She watched me."

"My stepmother," he said thoughtfully. "We
should talk to her."

"I think we need to talk to Sally first. Make sure the woman at the party was really your stepmother. We can find out if she asked about the drawing or about me."

"I'm not sure we can trust Sally," Johnny said, studying the picture. "Is the baby my father's child?"

"Your half-brother. He'd be about four years old now."

Johnny looked at the picture a few moments longer. His half brother. A disturbing thought occurred to him. If he and his daughter were dead, then this child would be the only heir to the Yarbrough fortune.

He couldn't forget for a second that whoever had kidnapped Katie wanted him dead, and because of that, he and Paige and Katie were all in danger. His gaze darted warily around the room. "Let's get out of here."

SOMETHING WASN'T RIGHT. Jay had felt safe in the library all night, but suddenly he was jumpy.

He didn't like the fact that their pursuers had found them twice already. Fearing they might have planted a tracking device on his car, he'd abandoned it. It had seemed they'd evaded them, until the van had shown up right beside them in the middle of Canal Street. How had they found them there?

They'd evaded them again by going to the library, but the prickling sensation on the back of his neck that he'd lived with for so long had doubled, maybe tripled.

He urged Paige toward the stairs as the library began to come to life. Everyone appeared absorbed in what they were doing. Nothing seemed amiss.

But a warning tickled Jay's mind like the sensation

tickled his nape. He'd missed something, and he was afraid his carelessness might cost them their freedom, if not their lives.

As they stepped into the stairwell, Paige asked him, "Are we going to the Yarbrough Building now?"

Jay rubbed his neck, then his temple, where a headache was building. "No. Not there." He heard the stairwell door open, but it was just a middle-aged woman with neat gray hair and a briefcase.

"I just want to get out of here. Did you find anything on where they—where I lived in the archives?"

Paige nodded. "There was an article about your family home up the Mississippi Coast. I think that's where you grew up."

"How far is it?"

"About thirty-five miles. But Johnny, from what I saw in a recent article, Serena Yarbrough apparently lives in an exclusive community up around Diamondhead, Mississippi."

Paige pushed open the exterior door. "She's Chairman of the Board of Yarbrough. I guess she commutes the fifty miles or so to New Orleans for board meetings."

They walked out into the morning sunlight. Heat settled on them like a bright hot blanket. Jay liked it. He loved sunlight and heat and even rain. What he couldn't stand was darkness and close places.

As they walked across the brick terrace in front of the library, Jay saw two men out of the corner of his eye. He urged Paige in the opposite direction, hurrying toward a streetcar stop where he saw a car approaching.

"Come on, we've got to catch that car." He increased his pace and pulled Paige along until she was running to keep up. Angling his head, he used his peripheral vision to assess the men. Both of them had white bandages on their noses, and the smaller man's arm was in a sling. The picture they made sporting their twin nose bandages was almost comical.

"What is it, Johnny?" Paige asked.

He took her arm. "Don't look back. Hurry."

The streetcar was just pulling away. Jay grabbed Paige and lifted her into the car. He swung up into it as it rolled away, its wheels clattering on the metal tracks.

As he fumbled for change, he saw the two men running toward the car. The beefy guy reached behind his back, but apparently thought better of pulling his gun out in the open.

"Where does this car go?" he asked, still watching the two guys as Paige sat down.

"I think it's heading out toward Carrollton," she said, following his gaze. "Are those the same men? I thought you shot one of them."

A woman with a toddler sent an alarmed look their way.

He leaned close to her ear. "Careful what you say. Watch for a rental car place."

She grabbed his sleeve. "Are they the men who followed me?"

He looked down at her, then sat beside her. "Yes. One had his arm in a sling, and both of them have bandages on their noses."

Paige raised a brow. "That should make them easy to spot."

"That's what I was thinking."

Paige's mouth lifted in a tiny smile and Jay's insides twisted. She'd had so little to smile about. For an instant the cloud of worry lifted just slightly and she looked like an angel. It reminded him of her face from his dreams.

But her smile faded, and she frowned, considering something. "If we rent a car, won't they be able to trace us?" she asked.

He rubbed his temple. "Only to the rental car agency. We're not going to file a trip plan."

"You don't have to be sarcastic."

His head pounded. They'd found them again. He needed to think, but his brain wasn't cooperating. "Sorry," he muttered.

"Where are we going to go? We can't just keep running. Look." She held out the cell phone. "The battery is half gone. They said I—" She stopped on a dry little sob. "They said I only had until the battery ran down."

"I know. Don't worry. We'll think of something."

The cell phone. In the bright sunlight he could see crystalline droplets on the case. He stared at it, frowning. The tiny droplets looked like glue.

He stared at the shiny little beads as his tired brain processed the information.

Glue. Someone had used instant glue on the phone. Why? Had they glued the buttons just to make the phone useless except as a one-way communication device? It was impossible to dial out, impossible to open it up, and impossible to turn it off. Or was it something more than just a phone?

Paige looked back toward where they'd left the men behind.

"How do they keep finding us?" she muttered.

Johnny grimly took the phone from her and picked at a fleck of glue with his fingernail.

She followed his fingers then raised her gaze to his. He watched her face change as the realization that had already come to him dawned.

He nodded. "The phone."

Chapter Seven

Paige used her credit card to rent a car. While she signed the papers and deflected questions from the friendly agent about where they were going, Johnny walked across the street to a hardware store.

When he got back, he was stuffing a small bag into the pocket of his windbreaker.

"Let's go," he said. "Since you rented the car, you drive."

Paige got in on the driver's side and started the car. "Where are we going?"

"First to a restaurant. I'm starving."

She almost smiled. Right then he'd sounded like the Johnny she'd known so long ago.

"Any particular direction?"

"Yeah. Head toward Interstate 10."

She turned the car toward the interstate and drove until she saw a small coffee shop. "How does that look?" she asked.

"Fine. Any place is fine." Johnny grabbed the printouts from the library computer and jumped out of the car as soon as she pulled into the parking place.

Following him in, Paige watched him walking and remembered the last time, when he'd walked away down Urselines Street. He still had the same easy grace. He was thicker, more muscular, but still lean and long. Once she'd known every inch of his body. Once she'd felt his lips along every inch of hers.

As he held the door for her, she had to steady herself against it for an instant. Her legs were wobbly. She'd have liked to attribute the liquid feeling to hunger, but she knew it wasn't that simple. His touch had always had the power to melt her defenses. Now he exuded power. Her mind fed her a vision of him coming to her, all that power unleashed as passion.

"Paige?"

She blinked and realized she was still standing at the door. Feeling her face heat up, she headed for a booth. What was she doing having erotic fantasies about the father of her child—her kidnapped child? She shook off the feeling. There was no time for anything but Katie.

They ordered, but when Paige looked at the huge sandwich, her stomach turned over. She wasn't hungry. She took a sip of iced tea.

Johnny glanced up from the printouts he was perusing as he ate. He nodded at her plate. "Eat," he said around a mouthful of sandwich.

She shook her head.

"Paige, eat." He reached across the table and took her hand in his, his thumb rubbing the ring he'd given her. "We don't know what's going to happen. Not even in the next hour. We don't know when we'll get a chance to rest. You've got to eat when you can. You have to be strong for Katie." He squeezed her hand.

Paige dutifully took a bite and chewed, forcing it

down over the lump that seemed to perpetually reside in her throat.

As she ate she watched Johnny, allowing her mind to venture back over the forbidden territory of erotic memories as she studied his features, the changes that time and trouble had wrought in him.

"You're very different," she said as she prepared to take another bite of sandwich.

Johnny finished his sandwich and wiped his hands on his napkin. "Am I?" He took a last swallow of tea. When the waitress appeared with the pitcher, he nodded to her. "Different how?"

Paige shrugged. "You were so sweet, so gentle." She looked at his corded neck, his broad shoulders, his callused fingers. "Now you're—not."

He was the man she'd once thought he could be, if he could ever get out from under the influence of his domineering father.

He raised a brow at her comment, drawing her attention to the scar that marred his hairline.

"What happened to you, Johnny?"

He pinned her with his sapphire-blue gaze. "I don't know."

Paige didn't say anything else, stopped by his intensity.

"The first memory I have is of river water closing over my head. My first thought was that I had to find light. Not that I was drowning. Not that my head hurt like a son of a bitch. I had to find light, somewhere."

He clenched his fist and his knuckles turned white.

"So I fought for the surface and caught hold of something. I hung on to it and stared up at the stars until the sun came up and I could see where I was."

His face had blanched, and Paige wanted to stop

him, to pull him back from the horrible scene he was reliving. But more, she wanted to know everything he remembered about what had happened to him. She needed to know what had made him the man he now was.

"It was a while before it dawned on me that I didn't remember anything. I was just relieved not to be suffocating in darkness any longer. Then I realized my head hurt like hell, blood was dripping down my face, and I was really cold." He shuddered.

"The only thing I had were the clothes I was wearing. The shirt had a monogram on it. The letters J-A-Y and a funny symbol. So Jay became my name. The label on a tube of ointment in the free clinic where I ended up gave me my last name, Wellcome.

"I had cash in my pocket. Not much, but enough to get a room. I took jobs working places where they didn't ask questions. And I waited for the people who had tried to kill me to come back. I knew they would, someday."

Paige's heart ached for him. So lost, so alone. "What made you draw the pictures?"

He shrugged. "I'd pick up a pen or pencil anywhere, doodle on anything. I realized the doodles were turning into pieces of the past, so I bought a pad and let my fingers tell me what my brain couldn't remember. Sometimes when I'd try to draw, my head would hurt so bad I couldn't see."

She reached out to him. He covered her hand with his for a brief moment.

"But through it all, there was this one vision. One beautiful face that eased the pain, that stopped the nightmares."

He paused, tracing her palm with his fingertip.

"Why did I leave you?" he asked, his gaze on their hands.

Paige closed her eyes and sat back, pulling her hand away. "You asked me to marry you. You gave me your mother's ring, and you promised you'd be back the next day. But you never showed up."

She rubbed her sore shoulder. "I imagined all sorts of horrible things. A car wreck, a mugging. I even imagined you might have been hit on the head and have amnesia."

He looked up at her with an expression so ironic and sad that it cut her like a knife.

"I'm sorry," she whispered.

"No problem." He pushed his plate aside. "What did you do when you found out you were pregnant?"

"I have an aunt in east Texas. I spent several years there before I decided to come back to New Orleans."

"And you never married?"

She shook her head.

Johnny frowned at her for a second, as if debating whether to ask another question, then dropped his gaze to the stack of printouts he'd brought in with him.

"What's this?" he muttered.

Paige tore off a bit of bread and ate it. "What?" She looked at the printout he held. "Oh, that's an article about Yarbrough Shipping reorganizing. It was a few months after your dad's death. I thought you might find it interesting."

He read for a few moments. "Interesting to say the least," he commented. "Yarbrough acquired several small companies and reorganized. Most of the companies were support or supply acquisitions for the shipping side of the business. But they also acquired a couple of technology companies. One of them was a small outfit called Data Sentinel.''

''Data Sentinel?'' Paige repeated. ''What kind of company is that?''

Johnny didn't answer. He took the hardware store bag out of his pocket. ''Let me see the cell phone,'' he said, holding out his hand.

Paige frowned at him, but he gazed at her steadily and she could read nothing in his eyes. ''Why?''

''I want to take a look at it.'' The scar at his hairline lifted his left brow just enough to make his expression faintly sardonic.

''No.'' Paige looked at the hardware store bag, a faint sense of panic beginning to stir inside her. ''I won't let you tear up my phone.''

''I promise it'll be okay. Just let me look at it.''

''It's my only link to Katie.'' She put her hand in her pocket and held on to the phone. ''She has to be able to talk to me.''

He nodded solemnly. ''I know.''

Paige's pulse was pounding so loudly she was sure everyone in the restaurant could hear it. He was lying. She knew it. And by the look on his face, he knew she knew.

She didn't want to let go of the phone. It would kill her to lose the only link she had with her child, the only proof she had that Katie was still alive.

But Johnny was sure that somehow, the phone was betraying them. It was the reason the killers kept finding them. It was only a matter of time before they succeeded in killing them.

''You're lying to me. You're going to destroy it.''

He just looked at her, his incredible dark-blue eyes mirroring her own pain.

Paige had never cried. Not since her mother died. Not when she'd read that everyone had given Johnny up for dead. Not even when she'd found Katie gone.

But now her very soul ached. Her heart felt shattered. The emptiness inside her throbbed, and tears welled up in her eyes.

She took out the phone and held it against her heart. She hadn't let go of it once since this nightmare had begun. It was her connection to her daughter.

Jay thought he heard his heart crack as Paige's eyes glittered with tears. She'd been so brave, not breaking down once.

Now he had to do the hardest thing he could ever remember doing. If his suspicion was correct, it was the only thing that would save them. He reached across the space between them and without a word, took the phone from her.

Her hand stayed over her heart and her tear-filled eyes stayed on him.

"I can't let go," she whispered in a small, pitiful voice.

In that instant, Jay knew two things. He knew without a doubt that he had loved her, and he knew he could never make up to her for what he was about to do.

He dragged his gaze away from hers to study the phone. He ran his fingers over the whole case, finding all the droplets of glue. He inserted a fingernail into the seam in the side of the plastic case, but nothing gave. Reaching into the hardware store bag he pulled out a tiny screwdriver.

Paige moaned under her breath.

He slid the thin blade between the front and the back of the case. He twisted his wrist, and with a crack that sounded like a gunshot, the back of the cell phone came off.

"No," Paige whispered. "Oh, God! Katie—"

Jay stared at the two halves of the phone, his gut twisting. He was right.

He looked up. Paige hadn't moved, but a tear had slid down her cheek, leaving a shiny path. Her frightened green eyes searched his face.

He shook his head sadly. "According to the article, Data Sentinel was working on a GPS tracking device that could be installed in a digital phone."

Another tear slipped over the edge of her eyelid and clung to her lower lashes.

"We've got to ditch the phone, Paige. If they're using global positioning satellite technology, they can find us anywhere."

He pulled some bills out of his pocket and tossed them onto the table. "Let's go. They're probably already on their way."

As they stood, Paige gasped and caught his arm. "Johnny, look, it's them."

He looked out the window. The dirty white van had pulled into the parking lot. He could see the twin white bandages on the faces in the van's dark interior.

"Come on." He scooped up the bag and the phone and headed toward the back of the restaurant. They walked through a door labeled Employees Only, past incurious kitchen workers and out the back door.

"Give me the keys and you wait here."

"No," Paige said hoarsely. "I'm fine."

When Jay glanced at her she lifted her chin. "I'm fine."

He crept along the side of the building until he could see around the corner. The van was empty.

Their pursuers had already gone inside. It wouldn't take long for them to realize he and Paige weren't in the restaurant. They only had a few seconds.

"We're going to run for the car. You ready?"

Paige nodded.

"Now."

They made a dash for the rental car. Paige clicked the remote door-locking device and they jumped in and took off.

"Which way?"

Jay was watching the door of the restaurant. "Toward I-10," he said, rolling down his window.

As they passed a pickup truck, he put the phone back together and tossed it into its bed.

"With any luck that guy will be heading back downtown."

PAIGE FOLLOWED THE SIGNS toward Interstate 10, away from New Orleans. She was numb, as if all the feeling had been drained out of her.

Her rational mind knew that Johnny had done the only thing he could do. Keeping the phone would be signing their death warrant. But her heart cried out that there was no reason to keep living if she lost her child.

A sob erupted from her breast.

"Paige, are you all right? Do you want me to drive?"

She shook her head. "I'm fine." She couldn't look at him. She was too close to the breaking point. And she wasn't quite sure what would happen if she reached it.

She took a deep breath, trying not to let any more

sobs escape. "I assume you want to find your family home."

Johnny nodded.

Her only hope of staying sane was to put distance between herself and her emotions by focusing on the facts she'd gleaned from the archives. "The Yarbrough house is located between Bay St. Louis and Gulfport, Mississippi, and sits across the road from the beach," she said woodenly, gripping the steering wheel so hard her hands ached. But she had to hold on to something.

"Paige, I'm sorry—"

"Don't!" She wanted to stay in the safe area of reciting what she'd learned. She couldn't bear it if he apologized.

"If there had been any other—"

"I'm not sure exactly where the house is." She interrupted him. "We may have to stop and ask directions."

She knew Johnny was staring at her, but she just kept driving, not looking anywhere but at the road. She thought about the house. "Are you sure it's a good idea to go there?"

He didn't answer.

"I suppose seeing where you grew up might help you remember something, but what if someone is there?"

He still didn't speak.

"Johnny?" She glanced over and caught his gaze. The look he gave her was somber and guarded.

"Oh my God. You think they might be holding Katie there." She put her hand over her mouth, but a tiny moan still escaped.

"Paige, it's a long shot."

She tilted her head in a brief nod and pressed her lips together. "But she might be there. We have to hurry!"

"Hey, slow down. You'll get us picked up by the police."

She tried to drive responsibly, but the idea that her daughter might be waiting for her only a few miles away pulled at her like a net.

They drove for a while in tense silence.

"Take this exit and get on Highway 90," he said. "It'll put us right on the beach."

Paige took the exit and followed the signs to U.S. Highway 90. Johnny was frowning, rubbing his temple.

"Does any of this look familiar?" she asked.

He shook his head without answering. He'd grown distant, remote, as if he were concentrating on something she had no part of.

She drove quietly, thinking of Katie. The numbness faded and her heart pounded and her jaw ached with tension as doubts assailed her.

"Johnny? Do you think we should stop and call the police? I mean if they're holding Katie there, and we go barging in—"

He raked a hand through his hair. "I keep asking myself the same question. But two things bother me. First, this has to be someone connected with the Yarbrough fortune. That's the only explanation for them kidnapping my daughter and forcing you to find me. That means we're up against all that prestige. All that money. And I have nothing that proves who I am. As far as the police are concerned, I'm dead."

Paige's easy compassion was stirred by Johnny's

flat tone. She was certain he was hiding a lot of pain under that matter-of-fact exterior.

She nodded. "And the other thing?"

"Whoever is after us is not trying to lure us to them. They're trying to kill us. If we go to the police, we place the kidnapper in a dangerous dilemma. Do they let Katie go or do they get rid of her?"

Paige listened to Johnny put her worst fears into words. If they made the wrong decision, she would never see her child again.

"If the kidnappers are the same ones who kidnapped me, and if my stepmother is behind it, I think it would be a mistake to involve the police before we know where they're holding Katie. Our primary objective has got to be to stay alive and free, so we can find our daughter."

Paige swallowed against the fear that tried to burst out through her throat. What Johnny said made ominous sense. She just hoped they could hold out long enough to find Katie and keep her safe.

Paige opened her mouth to ask him what he thought their chances were, but he was staring out the car window, his face a dark mask. He'd withdrawn to that remote place inside him where she wasn't welcome.

Panic spiraled upward within her. When he cut himself off from her like that, it was as if a huge chasm gaped between her and the rest of the world. Between her and Katie.

She gripped the steering wheel until her fingers cramped. Blinking rapidly, she concentrated on the road.

I'll be there, Katie, she silently promised her daughter. *You know I'll find you.*

"Stop here," Johnny commanded.

Startled, Paige pulled over onto the shoulder of the road. Her pulse quickened. "Did you recognize something?"

He was staring out the window at the blue waters of the Gulf of Mexico.

Paige followed his gaze, trying to see what had caught his eye. There was a decrepit bait shop and dock with a few boats tied up to it. It must have been there for years, an eyesore among the new bright buildings that had sprung up on the Gulf Coast since the advent of the casinos.

The bait shop sported a battered sign that was almost too faded to read.

"Lime's Bait and Tackle?" Paige guessed.

"Limey's," Johnny corrected her.

Paige grabbed his arm, renewed hope springing to life inside her. "Did you remember that?"

He shrugged off her grasp. "It's there, on the sign." He got out of the car.

Paige got out and squinted at the sign again. "Well, I don't see a Y. Why did we stop here?"

Johnny looked around, his eyes narrowed against the bright sun. He walked closer to the shop and stood there for a long time, staring out over the Gulf. Paige heard a low wail off in the distance and noticed that clouds were gathering on the horizon.

Johnny turned around and looked across the highway.

Paige turned with him. Set back from the road, away from other buildings, was a house. It was large, two stories, with square columns and a big laurel tree shading the front lawn. Plywood covered some of the windows. The large front yard had obviously been meticulously landscaped at one time, but now it was overgrown and shaggy.

"Johnny, is that your house?" Paige whispered.

Jay stared across the highway at the big neglected house as cars zoomed by. It was so much like the fragments from his dreams. Only the fragments had pierced his dreams with hints of blinding white columns, beautiful gardens and the scent of gardenias.

When had everything gotten so gray and run-down? When had everything beautiful in his mind turned ugly? He dug the heels of his hands into his eyes.

A voice called to him, like a siren song drifting through the dark muddle in his brain. Cool hands brushed his away from his eyes. He heard soothing words as a small, soft body pressed against his and the cool fingers stroked his face.

He blinked and saw the one thing that was still beautiful. The girl from his visions.

"Johnny?"

He reached out and pulled her close, burying his face in her hair. For three years, he'd dreamed of touching his vision. He didn't want to ever let her go.

"It's okay, Johnny. I'm right here with you."

The words sounded familiar. He pulled his head back and looked at her.

"Paige," he whispered. She wasn't the girl in his visions, she was the woman who had appeared at his door two days ago. The woman who had borne his child.

And he was still Jay Wellcome, nobody.

Sadness engulfed him. He banished it by filling his senses with the real woman he held in his arms.

Her green eyes, soft and full of concern, searched

his face. Without thinking of the consequences, he bent his head. She raised hers.

Their lips touched and her gasp mingled with his as desire streaked like a lightning bolt through him. He grew rock hard against her softness.

He kissed her again, urging her lips to open beneath his, urging her body closer. He felt her surrender, felt the tension leave her, felt her body mold perfectly against his.

He didn't remember ever kissing her before, but it was as if they'd been made to fit together. Nothing he'd encountered yet had felt as right as this one moment, holding her, kissing her.

He shifted, cautiously revealing to her the fullness of his desire as he deepened the kiss. Her mouth opened to him, letting him in.

Paige almost sobbed aloud as the currents of arousal swirled through her. She melted into Johnny's strength, letting him take her, mold her, mesmerize her with his kiss.

She had never forgotten the taste of him. His tongue and lips threatened to drive her wild. He had always surrounded her with his strength, his safety, his passion.

She reached up to pull him closer, to more completely enfold herself in his promise of protection and love.

A car zoomed by, honking its horn.

Johnny pushed away.

Paige swayed, shocked by the suddenness of his withdrawal.

He wiped his face and looked around quickly. "I'm sorry, Paige. I didn't mean to do that."

"Johnny—"

He held up his hand. "I know. It won't happen again."

Paige's empty arms ached, as did her heart.

"Get in," he said gruffly. "We need to check out that house, just in case. Turn around and pull into the driveway." He was frowning, pressing the heel of his hand against his temple.

Paige quickly did as he said, and discovered that the driveway circled around the back of the house. She pulled up close to the back door.

Johnny was already out of the car by the time she'd cut the engine. "Stay in the car." He efficiently surveyed the back of the house, then quickly and cautiously rounded to the front.

Paige sat there for a couple of minutes, looking at the white clapboard house with the long building attached to the back of it. Boards covered most of the downstairs windows in the back, just like they did on the front. The house looked closed up, deserted.

But if this was the Yarbrough house, there was a possibility Katie was inside.

Paige jumped out of the car and ran around to the front in time to see Johnny step up onto the porch.

"I told you to stay in the car," he said shortly.

She ignored him, stepping up beside him.

"Watch out. There are some loose boards."

"Do you think this is your house?"

He didn't answer, he just stood with his hands in his pockets and looked back out over the Gulf, a bemused expression on his face.

"Johnny? Are you okay?"

He looked down at her, his blue eyes dark and unreadable. He nodded. "I'm going in. You need to go back to the car."

"No."

He studied her face. "Then stay behind me."

He examined a window where the plywood had fallen off. Paige stayed right with him, following his every move. Curtains prevented them from seeing inside, so he stepped over to the door.

A brass mail slot and worn, rubbed-brass hardware spoke to the age of the house.

Paige waited, every muscle screaming for action as Johnny examined the bricks that surrounded the thick wooden door.

Standing close to him, Paige felt the new, increased tension that emanated from him like heat from a New Orleans sidewalk in summer. His brow was furrowed in concentration, his left hand kept straying to rub his temple, and his mouth was set and his jaw clenched. It was obvious this house stirred something inside him.

Her heart felt like it was about to jump out of her throat. "Johnny, hurry. Katie might be in there."

"Don't get your hopes up. The place feels empty. But if she's in there, then someone is guarding her. We have to be careful."

She hugged herself. Her eyes stung. Please, God, let her be here, she prayed silently.

Jay rubbed his temple, trying to massage away the pain that seemed to get worse and harder to bear with each moment that passed. He debated whether to break down the door and burst in, or to continue exploring the white bricks around the entrance in hopes of finding a key.

He couldn't tell Paige what impulse had made him insist that she pull over right at that spot, or how he knew the faded letter on the bait shop sign was a Y. But when he'd seen the old building, he'd had to stop.

Then he'd turned his back on the water and looked at the house, and realized that he'd felt its presence before he'd seen it.

Something had shifted inside him as he stepped onto the porch. An odor, a fleeting vision of a room or a piece of furniture? He had no idea what had flickered across his inner vision in that instant, but he was sure of one thing. It was connected to the house, and it was connected to him.

He knew this house.

He investigated the bricks with both hands, touching them, pulling on them, testing them to see if they were loose.

"Johnny?"

He closed his eyes for an instant. The guarded hope combined with fatigue in Paige's voice pulled at his compassion. She was pinning all her hopes on Katie being here. He realized, despite his admonishment to Paige, he was too. Because if she wasn't here, he had no clue where to look next.

Still, for the first time, he had something solid he could work with. There was something inside him besides loneliness, strange dreams and a punishing regret that he had nothing to give this beautiful woman who was depending on him to save her child.

Their child.

He couldn't stop now. He was so afraid the crumb of familiarity that he'd managed to glean would float away, leaving him with nothing. He had to hold on to that crumb. Maybe if he could hang on to it, it would lead him to another and another.

Maybe if he found enough crumbs, he could put his Humpty Dumpty memory back together again.

He started on the second row of bricks. His eyes studied the mortar as his hands tested each block.

The scraping noise alerted him just as his fingers felt the movement of the brick. His heart pounded. He pulled. More scraping, then a small shower of ground-up mortar.

He couldn't get a good hold. He pulled the screwdriver out of his pocket and inserted it behind the brick, half-afraid he might break the little tool.

Now he could slip a finger into the opening and grab hold of the brick. He slid it out.

Back in the recesses of the hole was a key.

He sighed, aware for the first time that he'd been holding his breath. He grabbed the key with two fingers and pulled it out.

"Johnny! You found the key! You're starting to remember."

Paige's voice was shrill with excitement. She squeezed his arm and reached up to kiss his cheek.

He felt her lips, soft and warm, against his stubble. He hoped to hell he was worthy of her trust. He hoped to hell she was right about him remembering.

But it had been too long. He'd lived for too long with nothing inside him but fear and loneliness. It was going to take him a while to trust himself, or his fractured memories.

He couldn't reassure her. He was afraid to even say the words inside his own mind, for fear the crumbs would scatter and he'd lose what little he had.

"I didn't remember the key. There had to be one hidden somewhere."

"But you stopped here. You went right to this house, right to that brick."

He cut her off with a gesture. "Let me go in. If there's a guard in there, he's probably going to be armed. You stay out here."

He slipped the gun out of his belt and clicked off the safety before he slid the key into the brass lock. The lock turned smoothly. He gripped the knob and opened the door.

Something moved in the darkness beyond them.

Chapter Eight

Paige cried out, and Jay grabbed her and pushed her aside as something slammed into them. He shielded her with his body. His finger tightened on the trigger of the gun.

Turning around, he caught a glimpse of orange fur as the creature disappeared into the overgrown bushes close to the house.

He relaxed, blowing out a breath. "Cat," he said. He looked down at his whitened knuckles gripping the gun. He was getting altogether too proficient with it. Another hairsbreadth of pressure and he'd have pulled the trigger.

Behind him, he felt Paige relax. He moved away from her.

"It probably got in through a broken window," she said.

"Yeah."

He turned back to the door, slipping the key into his pocket. He stepped across the threshold into the house and eased the door closed behind them, turning the dead bolt.

"Do you think there are any other animals in here?" Paige asked, eyeing the locked door.

"I'm sure we'll find out," he muttered. He struggled to stay focused, to stay aware of everything around them. His brain was threatening to betray him.

The house was cloaked in darkness because of the boarded-up windows, but even though he couldn't see a thing, Jay still had an overwhelming feeling of déjà vu. He knew he'd been here before. There was an odor about the place. A musty smell, certainly, from being closed up, but something else too. A mixture of the ocean, pipe tobacco and some kind of cloying perfume.

The combined odors made his headache worse and sent strange, conflicting emotions churning through him.

He felt nauseated and dizzy.

He tried to breathe, but the old suffocating panic was on him and he couldn't stand the dark stifling place a minute longer.

He sucked in a breath past the tightness in his chest and turned back toward the door, thinking of nothing but escaping the blackness.

Paige's fingers closed around his wrist. Her touch felt cool and calming. Thank God she was here to keep saving him from the hell of his nightmares.

"Johnny, what's the matter?"

He shook his head, forcing his chest to expand, forcing his spasming lungs to take in air. Wiping sweat off his face with his jacket sleeve, he looked at her sheepishly.

"I don't do well in the dark," he said hoarsely.

Her face was a pale oval in the darkness. "Because you were kidnapped." She slid her fingers down his wrist and clasped his hand in hers, squeezing.

"Do you want to go outside?"

He shook his head, ashamed of his cowardice. "I'm okay," he choked out. He took a breath. "Pull the curtains, and stay behind them."

She stepped over to the windows and pulled back the heavy curtains.

He held the gun ready, balanced on the balls of his feet, ready to react instantly.

His pounding heart thudded faster as hazy light streamed in the windows. The odors combined with what he could now see stirred a storm in his brain. His head throbbed in rhythm with his heart.

He clamped his jaw, determined to keep the punishing visions at bay as he searched all corners of the big front room.

Looking at his face, Paige saw his desperate struggle. She wanted to take him back into her arms, but she knew he wouldn't let her. He was expending all his energy to stay focused.

"Okay," she said, as calmly as she could. "Let's look around."

He shook his head. "You should go out and wait in the car until I'm sure the house is…"

Paige lifted her chin and crossed her arms. She heard his unspoken word. *Empty.* But she wasn't ready to face that yet.

"My child may be in here," she retorted. "I am not leaving."

Johnny started to speak, then clamped his jaw and shrugged. "Let's go then."

They walked quickly and carefully through the downstairs rooms. The kitchen was spotless, a few spider webs and some dust the only indication that it had been abandoned.

He opened and closed a few drawers.

"Johnny, the electricity isn't on, but there's running water. Do you think someone's staying here?" Paige asked hopefully.

"Don't get your hopes up, Paige. More likely no one ever had the city turn it off." He peered into a cabinet.

"What are you looking for?" Paige asked.

"A flashlight, matches, something to help us see."

Paige looked around, then went to the drawer she figured was probably the junk drawer. Sure enough there was a large flashlight and several packets of matches.

"Here."

Johnny turned. "How did you find those?"

"It's a kitchen. I'm a woman." She smiled.

He gave her a brief, dazzling grin that twisted her heart. When he did that, he looked so much like the boy she'd fallen in love with.

They moved through the kitchen into the formal dining room, then on into the living room and the den. All the rooms were completely and lavishly furnished. Even televisions and books were still in place.

"This is so eerie. It's like they just walked out," Paige whispered, touching a dusty TV remote control that still sat on a side table near a comfortable chair. "I can't believe it hasn't been burglarized."

Johnny frowned. "It may be protected by a security service, although I haven't seen any alarms on the doors or windows. Have you?"

"No. Do you think we tripped a silent alarm?"

"I think we'll know soon."

She felt panic rising inside her. "But if there's an alarm, that means Katie's not here."

"We knew it was a long shot," he reminded her

softly. "But in case there is an alarm, we need to hurry. Let's look upstairs."

She nodded.

Jay stood at the bottom of the dark, polished staircase with his hand on the newel post. He felt an extreme reluctance to climb the stairs. He couldn't explain why.

The feeling inside him was a mixture of dread and anticipation. What waited for him at the top of the endless-looking stretch of stairs?

He knew their daughter might be up there, and that all three of them could be in grave danger at this moment. But still he couldn't stop the feeling that churned within him. He didn't want to walk up those stairs. Something dreadful waited for him up there, and he was deathly afraid it was his past.

Paige slipped her hand into his. "Ready?" she asked softly.

Grimly, he nodded.

They climbed the stairs together, Jay taking strength from the woman beside him, the woman who had put her trust in him, even when she'd discovered he had nothing to give her in return.

He swallowed nervously as they reached the landing.

Paige stood motionless beside him, but he could feel her expectancy, her pitiful hope.

She looked at him pleadingly. "Johnny, hurry."

He nodded. He felt the same sense of urgency. Was their daughter behind one of the five closed doors along the upstairs landing? Four were lined up in a row across from the railing, and one was at the far end of the hall. Between the doors were barrister bookcases, their polish dulled by layers of dust. Jay's eyes went directly to the door right in front of them.

He was having trouble breathing. He squeezed Paige's hand more tightly.

"Okay," he said in a rasping whisper. "You wait here. I'm going to check out the rooms."

She didn't say anything, so he stepped up to the door and turned the knob, then pushed it open, holding his gun up, ready to shoot.

The room was dark, but the odor that hit his nostrils was unmistakable. This was a sickroom. The sharp smell of disinfectant couldn't mask the odor of death.

This time it wasn't just the darkness that kept him from wanting to go in. His head swam with strange, hazy visions that wouldn't coalesce into anything he could identify. He leaned back against the door, forcing himself to focus.

A hollow sadness took hold of him, hurting his chest and stinging his eyes. Behind him, Paige turned on the flashlight and shone it around the room, sending reflections and oddly shaped shadows skittering around. He scanned the darkness. The room was empty.

"Stay here," he whispered to Paige. Cautiously he entered the room and slid open the heavy drapes, suppressing a cough as dust rose from the dark material.

In the light from the windows, he stared at the sight before him. It was a little boy's room, with a dinosaur bedspread and curtains, and a few stuffed animals scattered around. It had been cleaned out though. There were no clothes, and empty spots indicated where furniture or toys had been removed.

Jay went back to the door, still overwhelmed by

the smell, still haunted by the feeling of loss. "How could a child stand this room?" he said.

Paige looked at him in surprise. "It's a cute room. What do you mean?"

"The smell. It smells like a sickroom."

Paige peered at him. "No, it doesn't. All I smell is dust."

Johnny shook his head and backed away from the door. "I'll check out the other rooms."

The next room was also empty. It must have been a guest room. There was no furniture, but the colors seemed impersonal, and there was nothing at all in the dressing room or bathroom.

The third room was obviously the master suite. Larger than the others, it had a sitting area and a huge dressing room and Jacuzzi bath. It too was unfurnished, but the plush carpet was littered with small things like bobby pins, makeup brushes, tissues, a man's tie. The type of things that get left behind when people move.

This must have been the room his father shared with his stepmother. Jay felt nothing. Not even a sense of grief for his father's death. Judging by what was taken and what was left behind, his stepmother had not bothered to take any of her dead husband's belongings with her.

He stood still, listening to the hollow creaking of the house. He had pinned so many hopes on finding his family's home. Not only for himself, but for Paige. Now his hopes were dashed.

He'd been right, even if Paige hadn't accepted it yet. The house was empty. Katie wasn't here.

Jay's only chance to save Katie was to break down the barrier in his brain. If he could remember his past, could remember something about his own kidnapping, then maybe he could discover a clue that would lead them to their daughter.

"Johnny?"

Paige's voice, coming from the other side of the house alarmed him. When had she left his side? He hurried down the hall to the last room.

She stood in the doorway.

"Paige? What is it?"

"She's not here, is she?" Her voice was small and sad, her eyes wide and haunted.

He shook his head, dropping his gaze.

She swayed, hugging herself, her face going pale. "Why not?" she muttered. "Why isn't she here? What have they done with my baby?"

Her voice was becoming shrill and hysterical.

Jay tucked his gun away and moved toward her, wrapping his arms around her. She didn't relax at all. She stayed knotted up, hugging herself, her small body as taut as a bowstring.

"We're going to find her, Paige. We are. But you've got to help me. You've got to stay strong, for Katie. We're closer than we've ever been." He held her, comforting her like she had comforted him.

He wrapped his hand around her nape, and pressed kisses against her hair and ear and neck, murmuring reassuring words. She stayed stiff, and he just held on to her. Holding her helped him too.

Paige couldn't stop shaking. She couldn't let go of herself. She was afraid if she did, she'd fly apart. Slowly she began to relax as Johnny whispered to her. Maybe she'd be okay as long as he was there to hold her together.

His lips moving against her ear made her shiver,

and the bowed tautness of her muscles and tendons began to relax. She finally had the courage to let go of herself and slide her arms around his waist.

"We'll find her, won't we?" she whispered, burrowing her nose into his chest and hugging him tightly. "Please, tell me we'll find her."

He pressed a kiss against her cheek. "We'll find her."

She sighed and pushed away from the seductive comfort of his arms. Katie was depending on them, and they had no time for self-indulgence, even if having Johnny hold her made her feel strong enough to face any challenge.

"You need to see this," she said, wiping her face. "It's your old room."

Johnny's hands caressed her arms as she slid out of his embrace. At her words, he shot her a wary glance.

"My room?"

She covered his hand with hers. "Come on. Maybe seeing it will bring back more memories."

As Jay stepped through the door, he was blindsided by an onslaught of confusing visions and emotions.

The room was furnished in dark wood, the colors were muted, brown and tan and rust. Sketches and drawings lined the walls, stuck up with thumbtacks.

Fighting a dizzying nausea, Jay walked up to the wall and touched one of the drawings. It was a picture of a thin woman reclining, her hand reaching out of the picture. The picture was signed with three letters and the Y-shaped anchor.

"Mother," he whispered, his head throbbing with pain, his lips feeling strange as they formed the unfamiliar word.

There were other drawings that disturbed him too. Several landscapes with moss-covered cypress trees and an old wooden building with a pier. Johnny stared at the building, his heart beating wildly in his chest, the hated claustrophobia building inside him. Confused about his reaction, he wiped his face and looked away.

He scanned the other pictures, observing the signatures. The oldest ones were childish, and had the name Johnny printed on the bottom in neat square letters.

He traced his finger over each letter.

Johnny. He mouthed the name Paige had called him from the beginning. Did he know that name?

It was a good name. *John.* A solid, dependable name. But was it his name?

He dug the heels of his hands into his eyes and slumped over, resting his elbows on his knees. A harsh sound escaped from his lips.

Minutes passed, and still he didn't move. Finally Paige stepped backward and began easing the door shut.

"Wait," he muttered, his voice muted. He pushed his fingers through his hair and wiped his face.

When he looked at Paige, she saw the grim determination of the man she had come to know in the past three days. He frowned, then straightened and stood.

Stepping over to the wall, he pulled down one of the drawings. It was one of the thin woman who was lying on a bed. The paper crackled in his hands. He looked at it for a long time, then walked right past Paige and down the hall to the child's room.

She followed him.

Standing in the doorway, he looked at the drawing. "My mother was ill. She was in bed for a long time."

Paige heard the anguish in his voice. She wanted to touch him, to offer him comfort, but that wasn't what he was seeking right now. He was struggling to fit together the jigsaw puzzle of his memory and for that he needed time and space.

So she waited, hardly breathing, as he explored the jumbled mess in his brain.

"I don't remember how long, but I know I wasn't very old when she died. This room always smelled like a hospital."

He shook his head and looked across the landing toward the master suite. "After my father married Serena, he started complaining about me wasting my time drawing. He said men should work in business, not play around with art."

The drawing fluttered to the floor as Johnny grabbed the sides of his head. He groaned.

Paige saw his face turn white as a sheet. "Johnny?"

"Sorry," he whispered hoarsely. "Headache." He swayed.

Taking hold of his arm, she guided him back toward his room. "Lie down."

He complied without protest, still pressing on his temples.

"Can I get you anything?"

He didn't answer.

For a while she sat beside him with her hand on his shoulder. His rigid body slowly relaxed, but he still rubbed his temples. She knew he was experiencing pain that was beyond her imagining, and there was nothing she could do to help him.

Her heart ached in sympathy for him even as renewed hope filled her.

This was it. This was what she had prayed for since that first shocking moment when their eyes had met for the first time in seven years, and he'd told her he didn't remember her.

She had guessed that it would be difficult for him, but it hadn't occurred to her that it would cause him this much agony.

Finally, his clenched fists relaxed a bit. She caressed his brow and cheek, wiping away the dampness. After a while, his jaw muscles flexed, his mouth relaxed, and his breathing evened. He was asleep.

She smoothed the frown from his brow with a gentle touch. If she could take the pain away from him she would. But this was something he had to go through alone. She only hoped that at the end of his suffering, he would find his past.

It was the only way they could save Katie.

SERENA JABBED REDIAL, breaking one of her impeccably manicured silk nails in the process. She listened to the phone ringing and ringing and cursed, using language she hadn't used in twenty years, since she'd run away from the trailer park.

"All right, Paige," she muttered as she lit a cigarette. "I'll give you the benefit of the doubt, for another two hours. Maybe you really are asleep." She smiled. "Or dead."

She jabbed another number.

"What the hell are you doing?" she snapped, when she heard the familiar twang on the other end of the phone. "They're not answering the phone. Please tell me it's because they're dead."

"You ain't going to believe what happened."

Serena gripped the phone more tightly. "Oh, I'm sure I will," she grated between clenched teeth. She knew that tone. She wasn't going to like what her brother was about to tell her.

"They ditched the phone."

"No, no. *No!*" Her voice rose on each syllable, until she was screaming. "She wouldn't dare! She wouldn't give up her only link to the little brat!"

"Well, Sue Ann, all I can say is we tracked that damn GPS signal all the way across to Lafayette. Turned out we was tracking a Cajun fisherman in an old pickup truck."

"You incompetent idiot!" Serena coughed, spewing cigarette smoke everywhere. "I have had it with you. You're not getting one extra cent. Not a cent, do you understand? You can go back to Minnow Creek, Mississippi, and rot for all I care."

"Yeah, you'd like that wouldn't you? Then I wouldn't be a threat to you. Don't forget, little sister, I know everything you've done. You owe me. You never would have figured out that trick with old Madison's heart medicine without me."

"Oh, please. I knew all about that. I was just waiting for the right time. Now could we get back to the current problem?"

"Don't worry, Sue Ann, I got an idea."

She snorted. "Great. You have an idea. Congratulations on your first original thought."

"You'd better be nice to me, sis. I'm planning to deliver the happy couple to you."

Serena relaxed minutely and smiled. "I love it

when you sound confident. What are you planning to do?''

''You don't worry about that. You just take care of the kid. They're still going to be looking for her. And if I'm right, they're probably getting pretty close.''

Serena lit another cigarette off the burning end of the first and rang for her maid to bring her son to her room. She had decided they should order in pizza, before she had to go make sure the guards watching Johnny's little brat were doing their job.

JOHNNY WAS DYING. He understood that. What he didn't understand was why they'd picked him. He'd been attacked and knocked out as he was unlocking his car after having dinner out. The last thing he'd seen were men in dark masks.

Everything afterward was darkness. He'd been kept in the dark, starved for food and light for who knew how long. The only stimulation he'd had was sound, so he'd concentrated, memorizing each one, no matter how faint, until he could hum along with the eerie whistling of the wind through the building, the creak of the wooden boards as they rubbed against the steel rails, or the low faraway wail of the trains.

He knew when a mouse or a roach came near him. Sometimes he would rock his weight against the walls of the wooden crate that was his prison, just to hear it squeak. If he angled his head just right at exactly the right time, he could catch a glimpse of light through the cracks in the boards.

He knew by the sound of footsteps whether it was the big man, the little guy or the woman who approached.

He didn't like it when the woman came. She whispered things to a third man who always accompanied her. The third man had a backwoods twang that reminded Johnny of someone. And he liked to taunt Johnny.

"Your daddy must not care too much if you live or die. He's refusing to pay the ransom," the guy would say.

Or "how does it feel to know your money can't help you now?" Or "your old man's just leaving you here to rot, ain't he? And you thought he'd rescue you."

Johnny never spoke after the first futile days. He had shouted until he was hoarse, until he had no voice left. He'd beaten and kicked and scratched at the wooden crate until his fingers were bloody and his body was a mass of painful bruises.

Finally he just listened, and wondered. Had his father refused to pay the ransom? Johnny knew his dad had always been disappointed in him, but he'd never thought he'd abandon him. It took him a long, long time to accept that the kidnappers were right and his dad was never coming to rescue him.

It wasn't like he couldn't have found him. Johnny knew where he was, and knowing just increased the torture. He was in an old freight warehouse less than a mile from his home. It was on Bayou Lesgensfou, which hooked around to the back of the Yarbrough property.

He'd loved to play there as a kid. He'd sneak out and go to his secret hiding place inside the old railroad car that sat on steel rails inside the building.

The railroad ran nearby and he could hear its whistle blow. The pilings on the front of the warehouse would move with the water, rubbing the wooden floors against the steel rails, creating an eerie screeching sound.

The wind would whistle through the top of the building, sounding like ghosts crying.

Those were the sounds that kept him sane.

Long after he'd lost any sense of time, he'd been pulled out of the box. He was too weak to stand. He'd lost so much weight his pants hung precariously from his hipbones. His eyes were so sensitive to light he couldn't open them.

For a heartbreaking instant, he'd thought it was his father come to rescue him, but then he'd been thrown into the trunk of a car and transported for miles. When the trunk was opened, he'd tried to climb out, only to hear a sharp report and feel something hard and hot slam into his head.

He didn't remember much after that, until the shock of hitting the water revived him to full consciousness. As the water closed over his head and he ran out of breath, his body began to fight death, although his brain was ready to accept it.

Paige! he screamed silently, for the thousandth or the millionth time, as water began to choke him. *I never stopped looking for you.*

Chapter Nine

"It's okay, Johnny. I'm right here." A familiar and beloved voice jerked him back from his dark, watery grave.

He opened his eyes. Candles were burning all around him. *What the hell?* Where was he? And how did he end up here, dry and alive?

He peered at the room in the flickering light from the candles and realized he was back at home, in his room. He closed his eyes and breathed deeply, still trying to rid his brain of the suffocating panic, trying to clear his nostrils of the choking, dirty taste of the water. He coughed.

A soft cool hand brushed his brow.

"You're safe now. You were having a bad dream."

He sat up and looked at the blond vision lying beside him on the bed. In the soft flickering candlelight she looked like an angel, wrapped in white.

He knew her. She was the last thing he'd seen before he'd drowned, and now she was the first thing he'd seen upon awakening.

"What are you doing here?" he asked in wonder, his gaze taking in her long damp hair and his terry-cloth robe from the hook on the bathroom door and wrapped around her small body.

She was different, yet not. He stared at her, trying to make sense of the overlaying images that swam in front of his eyes like double vision.

She smiled shyly. ''I didn't want to be by myself. So after you went to sleep, I took a shower and then crawled in here beside you.''

''What happened? How did you get here? Where have you been?'' He frowned. The questions didn't sound right. He should know these things.

Paige's gaze was wide and wary. ''Johnny? What were you dreaming?''

He shook his head and leaned back against the headboard. He held out his arm for Paige to snuggle up against him like she always had, but she didn't. She just sat up in bed, pulled the collar of the robe more tightly under her chin, and watched him.

''I dreamed I was in a dark box. I was starving. I couldn't see.'' His heart started pounding and his head hurt. He rubbed his temple. ''My father wouldn't pay the ransom. He didn't care. He left me alone in there—''

''Oh, Johnny,'' she said. ''Your father didn't abandon you. He loved you.''

''He left me alone.'' His voice wavered. He sounded pathetic, but he couldn't help it. The memories were sketchy, confusing, but that twangy voice echoed all around him, telling him his father hadn't cared. ''He wouldn't pay the ransom.''

''No, Johnny. Look at this book. It was sitting here on your bedside table.'' She reached across him and picked it up. ''There's a note tucked inside. It's from your father.''

"My father." He took it. "He hated me spending my time drawing. This must have been my book," he said. "Great Twentieth-Century Artists." He opened it and the slip of paper almost fell out before he caught it.

He squinted at it then held it close to a candle.

"Dear Son," he read. "You should be reading this after my death, instead of me writing it after yours..." Johnny's voice faded.

Paige put her hand over her mouth.

"This book is the birthday present I never got to give you. There were so many things I never did. I never told you how proud I was of the drawing you did of your mother for me. I listened to your stepmother instead of to you. I know now that she deliberately tried to poison my mind about you. If it weren't for Brandon, I'd divorce her today. But Johnny, you're my—" He stopped, his head bent over the paper.

Paige took it from his unmoving fingers and continued reading by the candlelight. "Johnny, you're my son. I'd give my life to have you back alive and safe. Oh dear God please tell my boy I love him and I'll always miss him."

Johnny closed his eyes as the words swirled around him. The chill, the horrible stomach pains and headaches, the unrelenting darkness, tried to suck him in again. The twangy voice echoed through his head, but the words from his father's letter echoed louder. He began to shake.

"He tried to save me. He loved me." He took a sharp breath. "It wasn't a dream," he whispered, clenching his fists. "I was dying."

Not a dream. The words helped him ground himself in the present. He lifted his gaze to hers. "It was a memory. They really tried to kill me."

Paige's gaze was riveted on his face. She nodded slowly.

"I didn't know who I was. I'd been shot in the head." He touched the scar. "I thought I was a criminal." He took a long, shaky breath before continuing. "I hid."

"For three years," she said. "Do you know who you are now?"

He frowned. "I'm John Yarbrough."

Her face changed, seemed to light from within, although her eyes remained wary. "Do you know who I am?"

"I think so." He nodded, and he realized he did. The overlaying images merged, and he knew that the lovely vision that had given him hope the whole time he was lost was Paige.

After all this time, he'd found her.

Or had he? He had a fleeting vision of opening a door and seeing her there. Maybe she had found him.

"Oh, Johnny."

He was still shaking when she leaned over and put her hand on the side of his face. "I am so glad you're back."

"Paige, what are you doing here? I'm not sure what's happening—" He couldn't go on. Confusion twisted his tongue.

"I know. But everything's going to be okay. You know who you are now."

He took the slip of paper and tucked it carefully inside the art book.

"I know who I am now," he repeated, still confused. The past and the present were getting all mixed up in his brain. "What are we doing here?"

Paige frowned and watched him. "We're looking for my daughter. Our daughter."

Our daughter. "You found me."

"And you helped me."

"This is my room. My home." He took in the dark paneled room, with the stacks of books and closets full of clothes. It was as if he'd only left yesterday. A shirt hung on the bedpost, where he'd tossed it. A half-drunk bottle of water sat on the bedside table.

It was a surreal experience, to see his room looking like yesterday, when in fact it had been three years. His head ached. There was so much he didn't understand.

"Somebody's after us." His mouth formed the words before his brain consciously knew it.

Paige nodded. "They've been trying to kill us. So far we've managed to stay one step ahead of them. But now we don't have the cell phone and I'm so scared I'll never see my baby again."

He wasn't sure what she was talking about. He was still a little uncertain how they'd ended up here, but he heard the rising panic in her voice, and he knew that she, like he, needed reassurance. Someone to depend on, someone to share the fear and the darkness. Someone to hold.

He put out his hand and touched her cheek. She held his gaze as his palm cupped her face. Her fingers tightened on the neck of the terry-cloth robe and her eyes drifted closed as her head inclined toward the warmth of his hand.

He leaned over and touched her mouth with his.

The contact startled her. Her eyes flew open and she gasped, her warm breath whispering across his skin.

As the vision continued to meld with the reality of her, he kissed her tentatively, teasing her lips to open.

She hesitated for a moment, pulling back slightly, and for an instant he froze, remaining still so as not to frighten her. Then he reached for her mouth with his again, not releasing her from the kiss this time, moving with her, urging her gently back until she lay beneath him with his length pressed against hers.

Something was driving him, something beyond physical desire. He needed her on a level he'd never experienced before. It was a desperate, frightening thing, this need, as if he was striving to prove he was still alive, still a man, still worthy of her.

He took refuge in the warm, delicious recesses of her mouth, loving the taste, the feel of her. When at long last she wrapped her arms around his neck and pulled him closer, his sense of relief was so sharp it startled him. He made a low involuntary sound deep in his throat.

Placing his hands on either side of her face, he kissed her again and again, feeding on her sweet taste, on her beauty, on her soft, tender strength. He'd always been in awe of her quiet determination. He'd loved her more than his life.

"I thought I'd never see you again, except in my dreams," he whispered.

"I thought you were dead." Her lips moved against his skin as he buried his head in the curve of her neck and he breathed in her familiar scent. His body grew and hardened until he thought he could come just from being close to her.

Paige felt Johnny's desperation in the strength of

his embrace. She'd felt that kind of urgency from him only once before, the night before he'd left her. For a brief instant, the memory of him walking away overwhelmed her, but then his tongue dipped into her mouth and teased hers, and she forgot everything but his caresses.

His fingers caught in her hair, and he spread it out around her. "When did your hair get so long?" he asked, his lips moving against hers.

"I haven't cut it since you left."

He raised his head, frowning down at her, about to speak, but she lifted her face to his and he took her mouth in another breath-stealing kiss.

His kiss had always had the power to melt her, the way his hard lips became gentle and teasing, the way his tongue tasted her as if she were offering him sweet wine, the way the stubble on his cheeks scraped against her sensitive skin.

He moved away from her mouth to nibble at the underside of her chin, and his fingers, still tangled in the long strands of her hair, pushed at the edges of the terry-cloth robe.

Paige arched when his fingers touched her breast, cupping it, his thumb caressing the sensitive tip. It had been so long. No hands had ever touched her but Johnny's. No mouth. She had almost forgotten the ecstasy he could coax from her with just a touch.

He leaned back and slowly spread the robe open, gazing on her body as if he'd never seen it before. He glanced at her face, searching it, then shook his head as if he were arguing with himself.

Bending over her, he touched his tongue to the tip of her breast and Paige almost went over the edge. She gasped and pulled his head closer. His warm mouth sucked the entire areola in, then slowly let it go. Then he did it again, this time running his tongue around it and nipping the distended tip with his teeth.

Paige nearly screamed in exquisite pleasure. He stopped, leaving her panting and about to beg. But then he turned his attention to her other breast and started all over again, until he'd raised her senses back to fever pitch.

She ran her hands over his muscled shoulders and up to caress the nape of his neck, where sun-tipped brown hair slid through her fingers like finest silk. She tried to urge him back up so she could kiss him, but he resisted her. He was in control.

He moved down her belly, touching her here and there with his tongue, tasting her, as his fingers played with her breasts, cupping them, caressing them, teasing them until their tips sprang up achingly. Then he slid his fingers over her abdomen and farther, until he cupped his palm between her thighs and slowly stroked her.

His touch was like an electric shock, singing through her with the bright hot fury of lightning across a dark summer sky.

He dipped into her with one long finger. He slid slowly in and out, his head resting against her gently rounded belly.

"Johnny, please," Paige gasped, squeezing her thighs together. If he didn't stop, she wouldn't be able to control herself.

He stopped.

Absurdly, she wanted to cry *No!*

His moist finger trailed upward over her abdomen to the little stretch marks that lined her belly. Those maps that defined where she had carried their child.

"What are these?" he asked softly. She felt his stubble scrape against her skin as he spoke.

Her heart almost stopped at his question. Her child. Their child. Didn't he remember?

Before her mind could travel further down that path, before she could find breath to answer, he began kissing each little mark, one by one, crouching over her, examining every inch of her abdomen, running his tongue over every millimeter, until she squirmed in frustration and the agony of remaining unfulfilled. Her body was writhing by the time she could speak.

"Come to me, Johnny," she begged. "Now."

He gave her that unfathomable look again, then shed his clothes and lay back down, his warm length stretched out against her.

She'd gotten a glimpse of his body after he'd showered at his apartment. She'd felt his strength under her touch. Now she devoured it with her eyes and her hands, relearning every inch of it. Where he had been slender and sinewy, he was now muscled. His leanness had turned hard, his shoulders were more defined, his abdomen rippled with muscle, his thighs flexed powerfully.

She ran her hands over him, marveling at the differences, exulting in the familiarity. Her fingers brushed the scar at his hip. It was long since healed, like an old surgical scar. For an instant, curiosity about how he'd gotten it pulled her out of her erotic haze.

But he dipped into her again, deeper this time, and the sensation of his intimate touch sent all rational thought out of her head. She arched against him, more than ready. As he lifted himself above her she moved to accommodate him.

Johnny let out a shuddering breath when Paige's fingers closed around him. He watched her face as he sank into her, afraid of what he would see in her eyes, afraid he wouldn't be able to last.

Her warmth enveloped him. She was so tight, so ready. And yet a shadow of pain crossed her face.

He stopped, ashamed of his selfish and abrupt disregard for her delicacy. "I'm sorry. I hurt you."

He started to withdraw, but her hands held him. She smiled, her eyes shining. "It's just been a long time," she whispered, pulling his face down to kiss him.

A thrill of wonder coursed through him as he realized just how long it had been for him, and just how much he had missed the perfection of her.

He made love to her like he always had, with reverence and care, because she was now and had always been the most precious thing he'd ever known.

PAIGE LAY QUIETLY IN Johnny's arms, listening to his even breaths. Little aftershocks of passion still echoed through her, slowly fading into a hazy, supple relaxation. Being in his arms again was like traveling back in time.

In Johnny's arms, she'd always felt safe and loved. She felt invincible, as if she could bear anything, face any foe, as long as he was there beside her.

She hadn't felt that way since he'd walked away from her all those years ago. She'd struggled so hard alone, making sure Katie never experienced the fears she had lived with all her life. Her mother had been too self-absorbed, too wrapped up in her own heartbreak, to adequately care for Paige. Maxine Reynolds had wasted her life and neglected her daughter because she was mourning for a man.

Snuggling into Johnny's side, Paige thought about her own life. She'd devoted all her energy to giving her daughter the security and safety she herself had never had. She'd made sure every single day that Katie knew how much she loved her.

Katie. She stiffened. A knife blade couldn't have cut any deeper. Her daughter was in danger.

The fragile cloak of love and safety that Johnny had wrapped her in shattered like rotten silk.

She slid out of his arms and got up, grabbing the robe as she headed for the bathroom. She wrapped the robe around her suddenly chilled body and held herself as the awful significance of what she'd done washed over her.

She'd indulged herself while her child was lost. She had forgotten about her baby, let precious minutes go by that should have been used to come closer to finding her. The hole in her heart left by Katie's disappearance threatened to open up and swallow her.

Glancing in the mirror, she was surprised to see her eyes brimming over with tears. Blinking, she dashed away the droplets that wouldn't stop running down her cheeks, and lifted her chin. This was why she never cried. She'd discovered a long time ago that crying did nothing but sap her strength and waste her time. She had to be strong for Katie's sake.

She splashed water on her face, and buried it in a towel. But when she looked back up into the mirror, the tears hadn't stopped at all.

A shadow appeared behind her. She met Johnny's worried gaze.

"Paige?" Johnny whispered. "Are you okay?"

His brain was still jumbled like a partially completed jigsaw puzzle, but in all the memories he could dredge up, he never remembered seeing Paige cry. The two lone tears that had spilled over from her eyes when he'd broken the cell phone were the closest she'd ever come.

To see her now, eyes wide and filled with distress, tears falling down her cheeks, broke his heart. She'd always been the most courageous person he'd ever met. That stubborn little chin, those flashing green eyes were what he'd fallen in love with. He knew what she was crying about, because the same regret and fear were eating at him.

"I forgot about her." She swallowed and he saw her jaw work as she tried to stop her lips from trembling.

He reached out carefully and turned her around, taking her hand. "Paige, don't do this to yourself. You've been through a lot. I was scared and confused and you held me and helped me through. We comforted each other." He rubbed his thumb over the ring she wore. "Nothing we did hurt Katie at all. You're helping me get back my memories, and that's going to help Katie. Now come out of the bathroom and let's get dressed."

She shook her head. "She's all I've got."

Her words struck him like stones.

He understood the depth of her love for her child. He understood the horror of not knowing where Katie was or if she was okay. But still the words hurt him.

He ignored the pain and tugged gently on her hand. "Come on. We have to make plans. I think we need to leave here."

"Let go of me!" she snapped, jerking her hand

away. "This is all your fault anyway. You promised me you'd be back. *Wait for me,* you said. *Never take off the ring. It'll bring me back to you.* Nice words, Johnny, but you never showed up." Her eyes glinted like liquid emeralds.

"You didn't keep your promise, so my daughter ended up without a father, just like me."

"Paige, I—"

"Since you're remembering things, remember this. Why didn't you come back?" She stood rigid, her arms hugging her middle. "Were you like my father? Married? Or did you just think better of your summer fling once you got back to your fancy house and life?"

He held out a hand to her, but she stepped backward, until she bumped up against the bathroom sink.

"I don't know." He shook his head, rubbing his temple. "I wish I could tell you. But some things are still kind of mixed up."

She uttered a short laugh. "I'd say that's an understatement." Stepping around him, she went into the bedroom.

He followed her. She moved stiffly, as if she were afraid to let go of her rigid control. He wanted to take her in his arms and comfort her, but she didn't want that.

She dropped the robe and began dressing with jerky movements.

"I don't know what happened to keep me from coming back for you," he said. "I can't even tell you what kind of person I was back then, although I must not have been much of a man. Right now, I can't think of anything important enough or strong enough to keep me from you."

She turned around, and he saw her lips tremble just barely. "I can think of one reason you didn't come back."

He waited, seeing the sadness in her eyes, knowing it was his fault it was there.

"You didn't want to." She bit her lip to keep it from trembling and wiped her face with both hands.

"Did I know you were pregnant?"

She turned around and stared at him. "No, why? Does that make it better?"

He didn't know what to say, but a part of him felt a wary relief that he hadn't known she was carrying his child. Was he just grasping at ways to assuage a little bit of his guilt?

"This is getting us nowhere," she cried, picking up her jacket. "I've got to find my daughter. I need to hear her voice. I need to—"

She stopped, her jacket in her hand. With an odd expression on her face, she held it up, feeling in the pockets.

"The tape recorder," she muttered as she pulled it out. "I need to hear Katie's voice."

Johnny stopped buttoning his shirt. *The tape recorder.* Of course. The background sounds on the tape recorder. He knew those sounds.

"Paige, let me see it."

She clutched the little metal box to her chest just like she had the phone, and eyed him suspiciously. "No. You're not going to destroy my tape recorder. I have to hear my baby's voice." Her eyes flashed like green lasers, ready to cut him in two if he so much as moved.

"I promise I won't hurt it."

She lifted her chin.

He knew what that meant. She didn't trust him, and he couldn't blame her. He held his hand up, palm out. "Okay. But play it for me. Let's listen to it together. I won't touch it. But hurry. We're running out of time."

Stepping over toward the door as if planning an escape, Paige took out the little minirecorder without taking her eyes off him.

If he could just touch her, wrap her in his arms and promise her they'd find Katie...but he had to be careful, because he didn't want to break any more promises. He didn't want to break her heart.

She pressed Play, and her desperate taped voice echoed in the air between them.

Johnny closed his eyes. He felt disjointed, dizzy. The raspy voice of the caller, the metallic creak of the steel rails, the whistle of a train, all were familiar to him. His head throbbed in rhythm with his pounding heart. He knew those sounds. He'd been there before.

"Johnny, are you all right?" Paige asked, turning the recorder off.

"Play it again," he said harshly, his eyes closed.

She rewound the tape and pressed Play.

The sounds echoed around him like they had during the long, dark weeks of his captivity. He swayed.

"Johnny?"

He wiped his face and met her gaze.

She looked frightened by his expression. He knew why. Inside him anger was building. Like a stoked fire, it had lain dormant, hidden behind the barrier his brain had built to protect him from the truth. But now it flared. Fed by his returning memories as a fire is fed by oxygen, his anger grew.

He struggled to contain it, to channel it into strength and resolve.

"Paige, look at me." His voice was harsh. He had to force himself to lower it. He needed her to trust him, and he'd given her so many reasons not to.

"We are going to find Katie," he whispered, hoping she understood that this time he was offering her more than a promise.

Her green eyes widened, and color came back into her face.

He nodded. "I think I know where she is."

"WHY HASN'T HE FIGURED out where she is?" Serena muttered, staring at the wooden crate.

"Hell, Sue Ann, he was blindfolded when we brought him here, and you never let him out in the light."

Serena sent her brother a disdainful glance as she stepped carefully around the desiccated shrimp shells, nails and other trash that littered the floor of the abandoned warehouse.

"Johnny may have been in that crate in the dark, but he knew where he was." Serena smiled, remembering. "That was part of his torment. He's the one that told me about this place and how he'd played here as a child. He'll realize eventually that this is where his daughter is. But I want Paige and him eliminated as far from here as possible."

She lit a cigarette to mask the rotten fish smell. "Why haven't you cleaned this place up?" she snapped.

Her brother sat on a folding chair, chewing. He still had that disgusting habit. He spat, then wiped his mouth.

"Hardly seems necessary. It's not like you're entertaining your bridge club."

"I don't belong to a bridge club, you nitwit. How's she doing?"

Leonard laughed. "The brat's doing fine. She had pizza again. I reckon that's all she eats. And she's tired of the movies. Oh, and she's still complaining about how dark it is at night." His voice mocked the child's whine.

"Didn't you get her that night-light?"

"Yep, Martin did. She's just a spoiled brat."

"Bring her out here. I want to talk to her."

Leonard spat again, then stepped up to the boxcar and turned the crank that unlocked the heavy door. He slid it open.

"Katie?" Serena called sweetly. "Come on out, honey."

The child stepped reluctantly through the opening, wrapped in the afghan they'd covered her with when they kidnapped her.

Serena eyed the thing distastefully. The child never let go of it. "Katie, I don't think your parents are going to come. What do you think?"

Katie rubbed her sleepy eyes, then glared at Serena. "My mom will find me," she said, jutting her chin up.

Her disturbing Yarbrough eyes glinted in the dim moonlight that slipped in through the high windows of the warehouse.

Serena shook her head. "I don't know. We keep looking for them, but we can't find them anywhere. Can you remember where your mom and dad go when they want to be together?"

Katie sighed, glanced at Leonard, then back at Serena. The look on her smudged little face reminded Serena of her stepson. Johnny used to look at her with the same expression of superiority. Serena suppressed the urge to grab the child and shake her.

"I told you I don't have a dad. My mom doesn't go anywhere with men."

Leonard grabbed the girl's arm. "Look, kid, you better cough up some information—"

"Leonard!" Serena snapped. "Get away from her. You're scaring her to death."

Katie rubbed her arm and glared defiantly. "I'm not—scared."

"Now, Katie, I know your mom told you never to tell, but this is important. We have to find your dad, so he can come and get you. We want to help you."

"No, you don't," Katie said. "You're mean. You don't want to help anybody."

Serena had to laugh. "Mean am I? Well then, since I'm so mean, suppose I send you back inside." She glanced at Leonard. "I hate to tell you this, Katie, but it is so important that we find your mom and dad, that unless you tell me where they are, you won't get any more pizza, or anything else to eat. Little girls who don't do what they're told must be sent to bed without their supper."

Katie shrugged, but her lips quivered and her eyes shone with tears. "I don't care. My mom will come. You'll see."

Serena nodded at Leonard and turned away as he pushed the child back inside the car and slid the metal door closed.

"Why don't you just go ahead and get rid of her? She ain't nothing but a liability now that they ditched the phone."

"No. You never think things through, Leonard. She's still our best bet. As long as we have their child, they won't dare go to the police."

She frowned at her brother. "But as I told you, I'd rather have Johnny and Paige taken care of before they get this far. Speaking of which, have you checked the obvious places, like that eyesore of a house on Highway 90?"

Leonard grinned, showing his stained teeth. "Just what I was thinking." He leaned over to kiss her cheek but Serena stepped backward.

"We still think alike, don't we, dear sister?"

Chapter Ten

I know where she is.

Johnny's words reverberated in Paige's head as she gazed at a man she'd never known before. Gone was the tender, sensitive artist who had loved her and left her. Gone too was the bewildered lost man who had let her in and protected her on faith.

In their place was a different man, a whole man, his jaw chiseled from granite, his sapphire-blue eyes hot with a leashed fury that might have frightened her once.

Now, in the midst of her anger and fear, it gave her a level of hope that she'd never before felt. Johnny was back. He was whole, and he was ready to fight for his daughter.

"Where? How? Let's go now." Her heart felt ready to burst from her chest. "Where is she?"

"Whoa, Paige, slow down." He caught her by her arms. "I think they're holding her in the same place they kept me. I recognize the background noises. It's an old abandoned warehouse and dock on a bayou near here."

His gaze clouded, and Paige felt him struggling with the memories.

She could imagine what he was seeing in his mind. She hadn't forgotten the awful drawings at his safe house. Those horrific black slashes that represented what must have been the worst of his nightmares.

"Oh God, Johnny. The same place where they left you alone in the dark? We have to go now," she insisted, pulling out of his grip. "Katie's so scared."

"Hold on, Tiger. I'm not sure exactly where it is. My brain's still all jumbled." He shook his head. "I've got to think about it. But don't worry. We'll find it."

She pushed her fingers through her hair, then began braiding it quickly, almost feverishly. Johnny paced, his eyes following the movements of her fingers as she quickly finished and threw it back over her shoulder.

"She's all right?" she asked. "You believe Katie's all right, don't you?"

He smiled at her, his harsh features turning soft as he studied her face. Stepping close, he brushed away a strand of hair that had escaped. "I believe Katie's fine. Of course, she's scared. But they let her talk to you. They give her pizza."

His words comforted her but there was an edge in his voice that let her know his anger was still there, banked, smoldering, ready to burst into flames at any moment.

"The person who kidnapped me, who now has our daughter, is waiting for me to figure out where they are. She's waiting for us to step into their trap. I'm sure it's driving her crazy, wondering why I haven't already shown up."

"She?"

He nodded, his eyes blazing. "My stepmother."

"Oh my God. Are you sure it's her?"

"I'm sure. Listen to this." He picked up the tape recorder. "Listen to her voice."

Paige listened to the hated voice. "I couldn't tell if it was a man or a woman with that raspy whisper."

"Listen to the accent." He played it again. "When she says *time is running out.*" His voice mocked and exaggerated the twang. "It's her. I hated that voice. She always brought someone with her, a man whose accent was much stronger. *She* never spoke above a whisper. She'd tell him what to say to me. I think I knew even then that it was Serena."

"I remember her at the party," Paige said. "She was noticeable because of her hair and that Dalmatian-spotted cape, but it was more than that. She was agitated, angry."

She thought back. "Seeing that drawing with your signature and a current date must have been as big a shock for her as it was for me."

She thought about the woman's eyes on her, the look of hostility that at the time Paige had interpreted as snobbishness. Now though, thinking back, Serena's narrow gaze seemed ominous.

"And then she heard you talking to Sally about Katie."

Paige stared at him. "That's right. That must be how she figured out Katie was your daughter. Sally went on and on about Katie's unusual blue eyes."

"So she naturally assumed you'd know where I was." Johnny laughed shortly. "She always hated me. I remember, she did everything she could to turn my dad against me. From the moment she came into our lives, she pestered him to get rid of everything that had belonged to my mother and to change his will.''

''He didn't put her in his will?''

Johnny shook his head grimly. ''After my mother died, he left all his money in trust to his oldest surviving child.''

His words sent a chill down Paige's spine. ''Oldest surviving child,'' she repeated. ''Serena has a son.''

Johnny's brows lowered. ''Brandon,'' he said thoughtfully. ''My stepbrother. He was just a baby when I was kidnapped.''

As he talked, he picked up his gun and ejected the nearly empty clip. The noise echoed in the room. He fished in the pocket of his windbreaker and pulled out an extra clip and checked it, then inserted it with metallic authority into the gun.

Paige followed his efficient movements in awe. The man Johnny had become was in many ways a stranger to her. The hands she'd watched create beautiful images on paper now held a deadly weapon, handling it with ease. He examined it and hefted it in his hand, checking its weight.

Paige spoke without taking her eyes off the gun. ''So if the oldest surviving child inherits everything…. Serena had you kidnapped and tried to kill you so her son would be the oldest surviving child?''

He nodded. ''That's the only way she'd ever be able to get her hands on the money.''

Paige processed the information, then fear squeezed her heart like a fist as her brain made the next logical leap. ''Her son is younger than Katie.'' She wrung her hands. ''Oh God, Johnny. She's going to kill Katie.''

He tucked the gun into his belt and faced Paige,

squeezing her shoulders comfortingly. "Listen to me, I'm the one Serena is after. Until she can be sure I'm dead, she can't afford to let anything happen to Katie. She knows the only thing that's keeping us from going to the police is the threat of harm to our child."

His grip tightened on her shoulders. "As soon as Katie's out of danger, all bets are off. We'll sic the police on her so fast her head will spin. In the meantime, she thinks she's in control of the situation."

He stepped back and punched one fist into his other palm. "My dear stepmother always underestimated me. She thinks I'm still the kid she had kidnapped. And she has no idea how strong you are."

"Well, then she's in for a big—"

"Shh." Johnny held up his hand.

She stopped, and listened. At first she didn't hear anything. But then a door creaked downstairs.

"Johnny—"

Johnny grabbed Paige and put his hand gently over her mouth. "Don't make a sound," he whispered urgently. "There's a door at the end of the hall. It leads to a back staircase. I want you to go wait on the far side of that door at the head of the staircase."

"But—" Her voice was muffled by his hand.

"Shh," he whispered. "If you hear anyone coming up the stairs…" He paused and looked around. His baseball bat was somewhere in this room. He spotted it on a shelf. Grabbing it, he handed it to her.

Footsteps sounded below them, as if someone was walking through the dining room.

"Hit the door to warn me if you hear anyone. Otherwise, wait there for me. If someone other than me opens this door, run. There's a latch about a foot above the doorknob at the bottom of the stairs. It's pitch-black in there. You'll have to feel for it. When you find it, press it toward the wall.''

He showed her with a gesture. "Push the door closed behind you and it'll lock again. You'll be in the servant's quarters. Run all the way through them. Hide in the closet at the back of the quarters.''

Paige shook her head. "I don't want to leave you.''

Johnny pulled her close and kissed the top of her head, then he smiled down at her. "Trust me. I'll come and get you.''

Her face pale, her eyes still glistening with tears, she tried her best to smile. Her faith in him awed and humbled him. He had no idea whether he could save them or not, but he knew he would die before he would ever let her down again.

He touched the corner of her lip with his thumb. "Don't let anything you hear out here worry you, okay? Now go.''

He stepped to the door and opened it a crack to peer out. The landing was wide, and nothing on the ground level below them was visible except the front entrance. Johnny didn't see anything moving, and at least for the moment all was silent, so he pulled Paige close and gestured toward the door that stood at right angles to his.

"Go now. Hug the wall so nobody downstairs can see you if they look up," he hissed, and gave her a push.

With a last panicked glance at his face, she went.

Johnny breathed easier once she was on the other side of the thick wooden door. All his life the door at the bottom of the stairs that opened into the old servants' quarters had been locked. He'd rigged the trip for the inside latch himself. It had been his secret.

He'd never told anyone. Not his father, not even any of his friends. It was his own personal escape hatch. And he'd used it often, especially after Serena had come to live with them.

It struck him that he'd always managed to keep a means of escape handy. Not only after he'd woken up with no memory, but before too. What did that say about him?

He still couldn't ferret out the memory of that fateful day he'd walked away from Paige. Maybe he'd been escaping then too? Maybe he'd never intended to go back for her. Had he been the kind of man who would do that?

There it was again, the one inescapable question.

He rubbed his temple, wishing he could make his brain give up the rest of his memories. But his stubborn brain only yielded a bit at a time, and not always what he needed when he needed it.

A noise turned his attention back to whoever was downstairs. Clicking the safety off his gun, he stepped over to the railing and carefully looked down.

Something moved. He jerked back. He'd seen a shadow below, along the edge of his field of vision. Whoever was down there was on their way up the stairs, and it wasn't a stray cat.

He listened for an instant. From the sounds, he could tell there were two of them. They were whispering, then he heard one set of footsteps head back toward the kitchen.

He glanced around, then looked over his shoulder at the door to the back stairs. He needed to stay as close to that door as possible, in case she needed him.

He backed up, gun pointed at the elegant mahogany

staircase, until he came even with the last set of barrister bookcases, the ones nearest the back stairs.

He stepped behind them. The position put him at a disadvantage. He was right-handed, but because his right side was against the bookcases, he'd have to shoot with his left hand or step out into the open.

He weighed the gun in his left hand, learning the feel of it. His finger wrapped around the trigger and he readied himself to shoot as he angled his head around the edge of the bookcase to look across the landing.

He heard a board creak on the stairs. Johnny tensed, his left hand awkwardly holding the gun.

A head appeared, but who was it? He didn't want to panic and shoot an innocent person. Then the head turned, and Johnny saw the bandage that decorated the beefy guy's swollen nose.

Knowing he had very little hope for accuracy, Johnny fired, hoping he didn't accidentally kill the man. He just wanted to keep Paige safe and rescue Katie. He didn't want to become a killer.

Beefy ducked, then raised up and fired in the direction of the bookcase. Wood splintered next to Johnny's neck, throwing a sliver up to scratch his cheek. He ducked back.

More shots came, peppering the bookcase and shattering glass.

Johnny switched the gun to his right hand. He had no choice. He was fighting for their lives. He needed to shoot as accurately as possible.

He stepped out and fired, holding the gun in both hands, wishing he'd taken the time to learn to use the gun accurately.

Beefy fired, then dropped out of sight.

Johnny crouched, trying to make himself a smaller target, and kept shooting. He didn't even know how many times he'd fired. The gun's magazine held ten cartridges. He had one more clip in his pocket. He hoped he wouldn't have to use it.

A shot zipped past his head. He flinched, then fired at the staircase again. He had to stop the two men any way he could. He had to stay alive, so he could save his child.

He wondered where Beefy's partner was, and if Paige was all right. The top of Beefy's head rose above the level of the landing. Johnny fired, and heard a grunt of pain.

Adrenaline pumped through his veins, burning, raising his consciousness to razor sharpness. His shot had hit Beefy. Had he killed him?

He waited, but nothing happened. He turned his head toward the back stairs, listening. Was Beefy's partner circling the house to approach from the back?

Something hit him, knocking the gun out of his hand and forcing a cry from his lips. Then he heard the report. He fell backward and watched his gun slide across the slick hardwood floor toward the railing. He dove for it, grabbing it with both hands, although his right hand felt like it had been slammed in a door. It ached, and was going numb.

Johnny gripped the weapon and concentrated on the stairs, refusing to allow his brain to accept what his body already knew.

He'd been shot.

Beefy's head appeared, and Johnny fired. A muffled cry rang out, then a thud.

He scrambled back over to the shelter of the bookcase, leaned back against the wall and waited. No sound came from the stairwell. He straightened, making sure his legs would hold him up, then crouched and crept over toward the head of the stairs. He maneuvered into a position where he could, by leaning over, see down the staircase.

Peeking over the landing, he caught sight of Beefy sprawled on the stairs, blood streaming from a wound in his head. Johnny's pulse pounded in his temples as he tried to determine if the man was unconscious or dead.

Suddenly Beefy raised his gun and fired. Johnny jerked backward, noting that Beefy's shot had gone wild.

"Who are you? Did Serena Yarbrough send you?" he yelled, aiming at Beefy's chest.

"Go to hell," the other man gasped, trying to pull himself up. He slipped in his own blood and grunted as he fell back down. He raised his gun again.

"No thanks," Johnny responded, dodging another wild shot that hit the ceiling and showered them both with plaster.

He left the man bleeding on the stairs and crept back to the back staircase door.

"Paige, I'm coming in," he said softly. He slipped through the door into the darkness, pushing until he heard the latch click behind him.

He squeezed his eyes shut, trying to rid himself of his odd lightheadedness and the feeling of numbness in his right hand.

"Johnny? Are you all right?" Paige gripped his shirtsleeve. "I heard so many gunshots." Her voice held a faint note of panic as she bunched his sleeve in her fist.

"I'm fine. Let's get out of here. The other guy's around somewhere."

He kept his eyes closed, pretending to himself that it was to stay oriented, pretending that if he opened them, he'd be able to find a sliver of light somewhere, pretending the darkness didn't bother him.

He urged Paige down the stairs in front of him, holding his hand out, feeling for the door. He hoped to hell that she didn't notice how fast and unsteady his heartbeat was. She stopped suddenly, and he bumped her from behind.

"Now let me go first," he whispered, her sweet-smelling hair against his nose. Eyes still tightly closed, he felt around the wall for his secret trip mechanism. To his relief, his shaking thumb went right to it. He pushed. The door clicked softly open.

Redness in front of his closed lids told him they had emerged into a lighted area. He opened his eyes, breathing for the first time since the upper door had closed.

The stairs exited into a long, low building, the servant's quarters attached to the original turn-of-the-century house. Johnny pushed Paige behind him and surveyed the dim interior of the quarters, alert to anything that would tell him someone else was here. The room seemed empty.

He carefully transferred the gun into his left hand, noting absently that his right hand had almost no feeling in it any more.

Paige squinted against the sunlight that filtered in through the dirty windows. The long room was filled with single beds lined up like barracks. About halfway down the room a thick curtain hung across the entire width. A way to separate male and female servants decades before? The curtain was open about halfway, but the sunlight faded into darkness down toward the other end of the room.

She turned her attention to Johnny, who was standing a couple of steps in front of her. His right shirtsleeve was dark and wet. She reached out to brush at it, not really comprehending what it was, and her fingers came away sticky and smeared with dark red.

A metallic odor stunned her.

"Oh my God!" she gasped.

He froze.

"Johnny, you're hurt!"

"Not now!" he snapped.

She grabbed his wet, sticky shirtsleeve. "Yes, now!" She tugged on his arm.

He grunted and swayed.

"You've been shot. We've got to do something."

He whirled on her and his face was pale but stoic. "We don't have time. Keep an eye on the windows."

He started down the long room, but a noise behind them stopped him. He reversed his steps and went to stand, feet braced apart, in front of the door to the stairs.

"Get out of here, Paige."

"No!"

Another memory stirred in his brain. An old house on stilts; puppies; a place where he was just Johnny and not the heir to the Yarbrough fortune. "Go out the door at the end of the building and run north. You'll come to an old house on stilts. Some friends of mine lived there. If they're still alive, they'll still be there and they'll help you. Miss Aileen and Mr. Woodrow. Tell them you're Johnny's friend and you want to see the puppies."

"Puppies?"

He nodded. "If you say that they'll know I sent you."

Paige straightened defiantly. "I'm not leaving you," she whispered, just as she heard someone bang on the stairwell door.

Whoever had shot Johnny had followed them down the stairs.

She gripped the bat with both hands, ready to swing, ready to do anything she possibly could to help Johnny protect them.

A scraping noise behind her startled her. She turned and saw a khaki-clad leg sticking through one of the low windows.

She opened her mouth to alert Johnny, but another blow on the stairwell door splintered wood. Johnny raised his gun and fired at the top of the door, a warning shot.

He had his hands full.

Paige watched the man at the window. He had one leg in, and in a very few seconds, he'd be inside. If he had a gun, they were dead.

She moved to the wall and crept along it, as quickly as she could, baseball bat raised. What she was thinking of doing nauseated her, but she was fighting for her life, for Johnny's, and most importantly, for Katie's.

Standing next to the window, she waited until the man's foot touched the floor, then she reared back and swung the bat with all her strength at his knee.

She felt and heard cartilage and bone crush, then an instant later she heard an ear-splitting yowl.

Feeling sick, she reared back again, doing her best not to let his screams shred her raw nerves. But her first blow had been enough. He fell backward out of the window.

"Paige?" Johnny half turned, checking on her.

"I'm okay. I got rid of him."

He shot her a surprised glance then turned back around to the weakening door. He aimed carefully at the middle of the door and fired. A surprised grunt sounded through the solid slab of wood.

Johnny turned around. "Let's get out of here while we can," he said.

They ran to the far end of the room where he found the outside door padlocked. Cursing under his breath, Johnny gestured to Paige to stand back. He shot the lock off. Then he pushed open the door and slipped through first, motioning to Paige to follow him after he'd made sure no one was waiting for them outside.

They had handicapped their pursuers for the moment. Paige spared a brief hope that the little guy in the khaki pants wasn't crippled for life, but she really couldn't work up much concern about him. He had shot at them!

Johnny stopped and pointed. "Why don't you go through there to Miss Aileen's and wait for me?"

"Wait for you?" Paige couldn't believe her ears. "You seriously think I'm going to let you out of my sight?"

He gave her a small, ironic smile. "No, but I thought I'd try." Then he became serious. "We could be headed into more danger, and you need to stay safe for Katie."

She touched the ring she had never taken off her finger. "I trust you," she said simply.

He narrowed his gaze, then led them around the servant's quarters to the driveway, where their rental

car was parked. The white van was behind it. Paige
ran for the driver's side of the car, reaching for her
keys.

But Johnny headed for the van.

"What are you doing?"

He glanced over his shoulder at the house. "I'm
going to see if they left anything we can use."

Paige followed him cautiously. Before he did anything else though, he pulled Katie's picture out of the
pocket of his shirt. For an instant he just looked at it,
then he tucked it carefully into his jeans. He unbut-
toned his shirt and shrugged out of it, leaving him in
just a T-shirt.

"Tear off the sleeve."

"Your arm's still bleeding," she gasped, staring at
the deep furrow the bullet had plowed into his skin.
"It looks terrible."

"Use the shirtsleeve for a bandage. Hurry."

She tugged on the shirt, but the cotton was too
tough. It wouldn't tear. Without a word, Johnny
pulled a pocketknife out, flipped it open, and handed
it to her. She sliced the unbloodied sleeve off the
shirt, then quickly wrapped it around his right forearm
and stripped another length of cloth from the shirt to
tie around it to hold it in place.

"Tighter," he grunted.

She obeyed. "Johnny, this isn't good. You need to
wash it. We need some antibiotic ointment and real
bandages."

He ignored her and tried the van's driver's side
door. It was unlocked. He climbed in and looked
around.

Paige went around to the other side and opened the
door. "What are you looking for?" she whispered.

"I was hoping maybe they were tracking us from the van, using a laptop or a handheld. But apparently the GPS tracking system is housed elsewhere and these guys really are just goons, doing what they're told."

He felt around under the seat and in the console. "Check the glove box," he instructed her. "See if there's any identification."

Paige opened the glove box and reached inside for papers. Instead, her hand encountered two plastic objects. She pulled them out. One was a flashlight. The other...

"Johnny, it's a cell phone."

His head snapped up. "Let me see it."

Paige handed him the phone and started rifling through the papers in the box. She turned up an insurance card.

She looked at the insurance card. "Yarbrough Industries," she read. "This van's insurance is charged to Yarbrough."

Johnny nodded, his jaw bulging with tension. "That's what I figured," he said, his words faintly slurred. "Hang on to that, we'll need it." He was holding the phone in his left hand and punching buttons with his thumb. His right hand was clenched into a fist, and blood was quickly soaking the crude bandage.

"We've got to get you to a hospital. You're losing too much blood."

He shook his head. "This phone isn't GPS enabled. That's good. We can hang on to it and they won't be able to track our every movement."

Paige looked at the phone. On the other end of it

was the woman who had kidnapped her daughter. "Can you see the last incoming call?"

He looked at her, a small smile of triumph softening the grim, pain-etched line of his mouth. "Yep. This should go a long way toward proving that my stepmother is behind this."

"Can the phone tell us where Katie is?"

Johnny shook his head, his lips compressed. "I doubt it. The most we could hope for is to have a digital phone company tell us which tower was used for the last call. That would put us within a several mile radius."

"Can we do that?"

"Not without going to the police."

Paige sighed in frustration. "Why can't we just call Serena and demand to meet her?"

"We can't afford to give her that much of an advantage. We've got to stay one step ahead of her, and count on the element of surprise."

Paige told herself not to be too disappointed. She ached for her child, but she had to stay focused. She had told Johnny she trusted him. Did she? She searched for the truth inside herself. She had to. He was Katie's father. No matter how he felt about her, he would do what was best for his daughter.

"So what now?"

"Serena expects me to show up at the place where I was held. And I will, but not in the way she expects."

"What do you mean not in the way she expects?"

He moved his arm, sucking in a swift breath. A shadow of pain crossed his face. "Let's drive up the coast a little farther. See if I can spot the bayou where the warehouse is located."

"First we need to take you to the hospital and get that arm looked at before you bleed to death."

Johnny closed his eyes and licked his lips. "We can't go to a hospital.

"Hospitals are obligated to report all gunshot wounds."

Chapter Eleven

"Oh." Paige looked at Johnny's blood-blackened shirtsleeve and his red-stained hand, and it occurred to her that he'd been through this before...alone. He'd know.

"Then we have to find a drugstore, because if we don't stop that bleeding, you're going to faint."

"Men don't faint," he muttered without opening his eyes. He tried to move his arm and grimaced. "Check under the seat and in the back. See what else you find."

Paige reached under the passenger seat, feeling around. She found nothing but some sticky coins and a couple of greasy wrappers that had probably held hamburgers. Then her hand encountered a folded piece of paper. She pulled it out. It was a map of the Mississippi Gulf Coast, open and folded to a particular section.

"A map," she said. "It looks like they were looking at the Bay St. Louis area."

"Bay St. Louis." He repeated the name as if testing its familiarity.

"That's fairly close to here, I think." Paige's heart

ached for her child. "Oh, Johnny. Katie could be near here."

"Let me see the map," he said.

She handed it to him.

He studied it for a few seconds, then lifted his head. "Listen. Do you hear sirens?"

She listened. "The police?"

"Yeah. Probably some good neighbor reported hearing gunshots. Come on, we've got to get out of here."

He got out of the van. "Start the car, and get it turned around," he commanded her.

By the time she'd turned the car around, he'd shot two tires of the van and was loading the last clip into his gun. He shot the other two tires and pumped two swift bullets into the radiator.

He ran around to the passenger side of the car. "Drive," he said.

She did.

As they pulled out onto Highway 90, she saw the blue lights of the police cars in the distance.

"Don't speed. Just drive normally."

She nodded, her hands clenched on the steering wheel. "What will we do if they stop us?" she asked. "You're obviously wounded."

"They won't," he said confidently.

Sure enough, the police cars zoomed right past them, probably headed for the house. They'd see the damage done by the gunfire and would find the two men.

"What will they do with the men?" Paige asked.

Johnny smiled grimly. "Those guys will probably spend the rest of the day answering questions. The police will find out they're connected with Yarbrough when they trace the van.''

"Couldn't they say it's the Yarbrough house, so it wouldn't be unusual to find a Yarbrough van parked there?''

"Doesn't matter. Bullets from their guns are all over the house and both of them are wounded. It means somebody at Yarbrough will have a lot of explaining to do.''

Johnny and Paige both relaxed as soon as the flashing blue lights and sirens were behind them.

After driving in silence for a while, Paige looked over at Johnny. His face was pale and drawn as he studied the map.

He looked wrung out. Her heart squeezed in compassion. He'd been through so much in such a short time. And now he was hurt and bleeding.

He glanced up at her, and she saw the anger she'd seen earlier reflected in his dark eyes.

"I'm sorry you and Katie got dragged into this,'' he said.

She turned her eyes back to the road. "I know. Me too. But at least I found out you didn't die. Even though—'' She stopped. *Even though you didn't love me. Even though you left me alone.*

"Paige, I hurt you, and I'm sorry. I wish I could tell you why I never came back for you.''

"I wish you could too,'' she said flatly. This man, this strong defender she'd known for only three days had remained at her side, but what about the boy who had loved her so long ago?

Had he even confronted his father? Or had he thought better of his rash marriage proposal once he returned to his big, expensive house and his privileged life?

She shook her head. "I think your father was very strong, very domineering. That last morning, you told me you needed to prepare him before you took me to meet him. You were just going to run home and talk with him and then come back the next day."

She looked at him again, but he was staring out the car window, and she had the feeling he was no longer with her. He'd retreated into that part of his brain where his fractured memories lay like broken glass. She wondered if he were finding more pieces that fit together.

Johnny's brain was awhirl. Images and memories were coming too fast for him to sort out. He massaged his temple and squeezed his eyes shut, trying to control his thoughts.

The message his father had written to his dead son explained a lot, but it didn't answer the question of why he'd abandoned Paige.

Johnny hated the sadness in her voice. He wanted to reach over and caress her hair and promise her he'd never leave her again. But right now, he wasn't sure she'd believe him.

He realized she had said something. "What did you say?" he asked.

"When you left, you said you were going to get your car and drive up the coast to your family home."

"My car," he whispered.

"I didn't even know you had a car. You said it was a Mustang. A Cobra."

He closed his eyes as a stab of pain pierced his temple and the fractured visions tortured him again.

Wet streets; pouring rain; a truck out of control.

Something silver rushing at him like an oncoming train. Time without meaning as he wove in and out of consciousness.

What was he remembering? Had he been in a car wreck? Maybe injured? Could that be where the scar on his hip had come from?

He wanted to squeeze his head, to capture the memories, but they flowed through his brain like a slide show out of control, making him doubt that he'd ever be able to slow them down enough to sort them out.

"Johnny?"

Paige's tentative voice stopped the slide show.

"Yeah?" He spoke harshly, impatiently. He hadn't meant to.

"Your arm's bleeding again. I'm going to stop and get some real bandages and some antibiotic ointment."

Johnny looked around. He recognized the outskirts of Bay St. Louis. And suddenly like a door opening inside his brain, he knew where the abandoned warehouse was. It was on the back side of Bayou Lesgensfou.

"Stop here!" He reached for the map as, with a startled glance at him, Paige pulled into the next gas station they came to.

A plan was beginning to form. A plan built off his returning memories. A plan to save Katie and keep Paige safe at the same time. But in order to accomplish both, he was going to have to leave Paige behind, because he'd already found out she would never agree to wait in safety as long as her daughter was in danger.

She had said she trusted him. But did she really?

He thought about her mother, pregnant and abandoned by a married man. How could Paige ever learn to trust him enough to love him again, or to believe that he would never leave her?

He knew the only reason she had found him was to save her daughter. He knew, too, that no matter what excuses he might offer to explain why he never came back, the only thing that mattered was that he must not have looked hard enough, because if he had, he should have found her.

"Do you know this gas station? Are we close?" Paige's hopeful voice tore at him, ripping holes in his conviction that he was doing the right thing.

He shook his head, trying to concentrate on his returning memories as he studied the map. He found the bayou road. He was right. The entrance to Bayou Lesgensfou was only a couple of miles farther east toward Gulfport.

The way the bayou wound back around to the west, he'd had no trouble sneaking out of his house and riding his bicycle through the back roads to the old warehouse where he used to play. Where he now knew Serena had held him hostage.

All those weeks he'd been less than a mile from his father's house. It had added to his torture, knowing he was so close to home. And now, his stepmother was holding his daughter in the same place, taunting him. He was certain of it.

He knew what he had to do. He just hoped he had the courage to do it.

"Johnny? Why are we stopping here? Do you recognize something on the map?"

He met her gaze and lied to her. "Take a bathroom break, Paige. We've got a long way to go."

"I want to get some bandages and antibiotic ointment and fix your arm," she retorted.

He nodded, avoiding her eyes. Her concern for him ate into his newfound resolve. "Okay. Just hurry. I'm going to put some gas in the car. Have you got a pen or a pencil?"

"I think so," she said. "I picked up a pen at the library. What are you doing?"

"I want to trace our route on the map."

She gave him a sharp look, but nodded.

"I'll need the keys. For the gas tank."

As she handed them to him he caught her hand, wishing he could explain what he was about to do, praying she would understand.

She smiled tremulously. That smile almost undid him. She'd had so little to smile about, and so much of it was his fault. He touched the corner of her mouth and leaned forward and kissed her gently. "You're so beautiful," he whispered. "Inside and out."

"Have I thanked you?" she said softly, her expression full of trust and caring.

He frowned and resisted the urge to pull away from her. He couldn't bear to look at her, knowing what he was about to do. Knowing that if he didn't survive, she might never know he'd done it for her and for their child. "You don't owe me any thanks."

"Oh, yes I do. You've given me hope. You've protected me. You helped me even though you had no idea who I was or whether I was telling the truth about our daughter."

"You found me," he muttered, massaging his temple.

She stopped his hand with hers, laying her soothing fingers against the throbbing ache in his head. He closed his eyes, drawing comfort and strength from her touch.

"Tell me we'll save her, Johnny." Her mouth trembled, but her voice was filled with steely determination.

He marveled at her courage. His heart ached for her grief and fear. He pulled her hand to his lips. "I promise I will die before I'll let them hurt either you or our daughter," he said against her fingers. Then he pressed a kiss into her palm.

He knew it was the truest promise he'd ever given her. He prayed he wouldn't have to keep it. He didn't want to die. He wanted a lifetime with Paige and their child.

Paige felt the press of Johnny's lips against her palm, and her insides quivered as she relived the feel of those lips touching her everywhere. She yearned to sink into his arms and let him take her away from the heartache and worry for just a few minutes more.

But Katie needed them. "I'll be right back."

Johnny nodded without looking at her.

A few minutes later when Paige came out of the bathroom, he was gone.

She stared at the spot where the rental car had sat, unable to believe what her eyes were seeing.

Gone. She closed her eyes, then opened them. She looked around. Maybe he'd pulled away from the gas pump and parked on the side of the station. She ran to where the car had been and stood there.

Slowly, her brain began to absorb the truth. Johnny was gone. He'd left her—again.

Her hands flew to her mouth. Why? She wanted to scream it at the top of her lungs.

Why? Why would he leave her now? Anguish

washed over her like a flash flood, almost knocking her down. Had he gone to find Katie alone? He'd asked her to stay behind, to stay safe. Maybe he'd thought he was protecting her.

But her mother's warning echoed. *You can't trust a man—* She did her best to ignore the voice in her head. Hadn't Johnny proven he was trustworthy over and over again?

Her mother's voice whispered, *You can't trust a man, it's in their nature.* And Johnny had left her before.

''Ma'am?''

Paige realized someone had spoken several times. She turned around to see the short, bald man who had sold her the bandages. He was standing at the door of his shop.

She ran toward him. ''Did you see the man in the blue Plymouth? Did you see where he went?'' Her voice was shrill and choked with fear.

''He said to be sure and give you this. He was in an awful hurry, but he made me promise to see you got it.''

It was the map Johnny had been studying. She grabbed it from the man's hand. It was still folded the same way they'd found it, but there was writing on it.

A small inlet that curved around to the west was circled and an X was marked on the far west tip of the inlet. A message was written in a neat, square hand.

Paige, you have to stay safe for Katie's sake. Wait here. If I'm not back with Katie in an hour, call the police. Show them the map, and give them the cell phone and the insurance card from the van as evi-

dence. I've marked the warehouse on the map. Trust me. And it was signed JAY in the familiar script from the monogram.

Trust me.

She had told him she trusted him. And she did. She knew he had told her the truth when he'd promised he would die to save his daughter. What would she do if it came to that? "It won't."

"Ma'am? Did you say something?"

She looked up from the map. "No, nothing." She spread the map out on the counter. "Where is this circled area?"

He leaned over and studied the piece of paper. "Why, that's Bayou Lesgensfou. Bayou of the crazy people. It's about two miles up the road."

Paige pointed to a line on the map. "Does this road lead back there?"

"That land used to belong to the Yarbroughs, back when they were a small shipper, handling seafood and fruit and grain. The road's still there. Don't know what's back there any more."

"Can you call me a cab?"

"Well now, your boyfriend told me to make sure you stayed here."

Paige lifted her chin. "How do you propose to do that?" she asked.

The man held up his hands. "Hey, I ain't getting in the middle of no lover's quarrel. I'm just telling you what he said."

Paige waited.

"Okay, okay." He pulled the phone toward him and dialed a number.

Paige folded the map and put it in her pocket, where the cell phone and the insurance card were.

She would call the police, but she had already told Johnny she was not going to sit and wait alone and helpless while her daughter was in danger.

And she'd meant it.

Chapter Twelve

Johnny drove along the bayou road, recalling his family's cook talking about the haunted bayou that ran behind the Yarbrough's house. Years and years before, the story went, a voodoo woman had lived back there.

According to legend, the creatures she had summoned from the grave still roamed among the cypresses, their keening voices carried on the ocean breeze.

Johnny had always laughed at Cook's stories, but secretly, he'd wanted to see a zombie.

So he would sneak out of the house late at night and cross the back of the Yarbrough property to Bayou Lesgensfou, partly out of curiosity and partly to prove to himself that the things his stepmother said to his father were wrong. He wasn't weak, just because he loved to draw.

Exploring the old abandoned shipping warehouse had filled many lonely hours for him. Right now though, as he drew closer, his palms grew sweaty and his heart pounded in remembered fear.

Up ahead was a sharp left turn in the road, and he knew that around that bend was the warehouse. If he was right about the sounds he had heard on the telephone and on the tape recorder, that's where Serena was holding Katie.

Johnny felt anger building in him again. He had reassured Paige that his stepmother wouldn't hurt Katie. But he couldn't reassure himself.

If she had subjected his daughter to even one moment of the dark, helpless terror he'd experienced, he might not be able to restrain himself. He wondered how many years he would have to serve in prison if he killed Serena with his bare hands.

The thought surprised him. Even with amnesia, he'd never been able to reconcile himself with the violence that the bullet wound in his scalp had suggested. Now he was carrying a gun and contemplating justifiable homicide.

He pulled off the road behind some trees. The ground was so soggy the car's tires sank into it, but he'd be better off on foot anyway. There might be guards watching the warehouse.

He picked his way through rushes and reeds that lined the shore of the bayou, staying in the shadows of the big cypress trees, steeling himself for his first sight of the building.

As he drew closer, the sounds he remembered from his weeks of captivity began to separate and clarify in his mind, until if he closed his eyes, he could believe he was back there, locked in the hot dark box, with nothing but the familiar sounds to keep him from giving up and going mad.

There it was, an old, stained wooden building with a tin roof. The sight of it stole his breath.

That was where they'd held him.

Quelling the nausea that churned in his stomach,

he looked back toward the south. Because of the way the bayou hooked around, his family home was only about a mile from here. When he got Katie out, he could take her through there back to the highway and over to the gas station where Paige was waiting.

He crouched behind a giant cypress tree, his running shoes soaked with swampy water, as he studied the familiar building. The front door opened onto a rotting pier where the shrimp boats and other small craft had unloaded their cargo. On the other side, Johnny knew, were the railroad tracks that actually originated inside the building, so that cargo could be loaded straight from the boats into the cars, then hauled off to market.

This side track joined the main tracks just to the north, and the wailing of the train whistle was one of the sounds he remembered. Every move he made, everything he saw fed his memories.

Johnny studied the area around the building. There were numerous car tracks in the muddy clearing, which spoke to recent activity here, but right now there was only one vehicle parked there, a decrepit pickup. Did that mean there was only one person watching Katie?

He sneaked around to the east side of the building. Sure enough, just as he remembered, a ladder led up to a window that opened onto a catwalk above the highest storage shelves.

The ladder was metal and coated with rust. As he quickly climbed it, he prayed it would hold his weight.

The inside of the building was as dark as a tomb. Johnny took a deep calming breath and grabbed the windowsill and lowered himself inside, into the darkness, his feet reaching for something solid. His right forearm burned with pain.

Finally he thought he felt something with the toe of his sneaker, so he let go, having no idea how far he would fall. He hit the catwalk with a thud and almost went over as one foot slipped. He grabbed at darkness and his arm hooked around a pipe.

The pipe screeched and gave, and he braced himself for a long drop, but it held. He got his other arm around it and hung on for a minute, until his labored breathing slowed. Then he swung his leg up and managed to shimmy back up onto the catwalk.

Only a few dim rays of light penetrated the high, dirty windows of the building. The air was still and hot, sticky as only a Mississippi summer could be. The smell of rotting shrimp shells and fish mingled with mildew surrounded him like a noxious fog, coaxing up the dreadful claustrophobia that he'd hoped he'd conquered.

He closed his eyes and listened to the whistle of the wind off the Gulf and the unique creaking sound that the pier made as it rocked with the water, rubbing the planks against the metal rails.

Fear churned in his gut and soured his stomach. He began to shake as a strange mixture of horror and relief warred inside him. He had learned to hate that sound during the weeks he was held here. But he'd also welcomed it. Each time he woke up, it was the first thing he listened for, because as long as he could hear it, he knew he was still in the same place, and still alive.

Wiping sweat off his face, he blinked and tried to control his rising panic. While he waited for his eyes to adapt to the darkness, he heard another sound out of his memory. The scratching sound of a match against metal. Someone was in the warehouse.

Over on the opposite side of the building, near the side door, he saw the spark of phosphor then the strong flame of a kitchen match. A small sphere of light illuminated the area around the man who hunched over the flame, lighting a cigarette.

Johnny didn't recognize him, but he hadn't expected to.

After the cigarette caught, the man held the match up to a metal box on the wall, grabbed a lever and pulled.

With a crack like the sound of thunder, the room filled with light.

Johnny dropped silently and instinctively to the floor of the catwalk, out of sight. He lifted his head just enough to take in the building in one swift glance. His gaze found the wooden crate where they had held him for all those weeks. The sight of that hated box sheared his breath.

He forced himself to concentrate on the man who was carrying a pizza box. He went directly to the old boxcar that sat on the rails in the middle of the room, turned a crank, and slid open the heavy door.

"Here you go, Katie. Pizza again. You got plenty of water?"

Johnny wished he could see inside the car, but that would mean moving, and he couldn't afford to attract attention.

"Did you watch the movies I brought you? Well, here's a couple of books, in case you get tired of the movies." The man stepped back and reached for the door. "I'll be here tonight, okay? So if you need anything, just holler."

Johnny heard a small voice but he couldn't understand the words. His heart turned over. That was the voice of his daughter.

"I know. I'll try to let you out for a while tomorrow, but I can't today. *She's* coming later, and we don't want to get caught, do we?" The man pushed the door shut and turned the crank, locking it. Then he went and sat down at a table with a sigh, and pulled out a bent and ragged paperback book.

Johnny felt absurdly grateful to the man. Obviously he cared about Katie, and he was trying to make her as comfortable as possible. He even let her out of the car when he could.

So Serena was coming. Maybe he'd make sure he had a surprise waiting for her. But first he had to rescue Katie.

It didn't take long for the man to nod and doze over his book. As soon as he heard the guard's snores, Johnny slipped over to the window and climbed out, skimming down the ladder as quickly and quietly as possible.

Waiting for the guard to fall asleep had given him time to think and plan. It had also given him time to remember all about the abandoned warehouse.

He had the perfect means to rescue Katie. But it would test the furthest limits of his bravery.

When he was a young teenager, the railroad car had been his secret playhouse. But back then, he hadn't been strong enough or tall enough to open the heavy metal door, so he'd had to find another way to get into the car.

From the underside.

He couldn't even count how many times he'd swum under the pier, through the dock pilings under the front of the warehouse, and climbed up into the car through the trap door in its floor.

Johnny stood there on the pier looking down at the water while dread churned in his stomach and self-disgust at his cowardice settled over him like a filthy blanket.

Could he do it? Could he force himself to enter that dark watery hell long enough to find the opening and climb into the railroad car from underneath?

The phobia he'd lived with since he'd woken up sinking into the black depths of the river. He clenched his hands into fists, then with a jerky shake of his head, he bent down and untied his shoes. He tucked his gun inside them and hid them behind the corner of the building. He took a deep breath, then another. With his heart beating like a bass drum in his chest, he lowered himself into the muddy water and swam under the pier.

The water lapping at his chin sent chills through him, even though the air temperature was in the nineties. He swam as far underneath the warehouse as he could with his head above water, but eventually, as he'd known he would, he came to a solid wall, where the extra pilings and supports held up the main body of the warehouse.

He stopped. He was going to have to duck beneath the wall and swim underwater the rest of the way. Panic streaked through him. The thought of the water closing over his head made him physically ill.

But this was for his daughter. The child he had fathered and never met, but whom he loved more than his own life. He would do it, even if it killed him. How could he do less?

He breathed long and deep, trying to slow his racing heart. Then, with one last deep breath, he plunged down into the black water, into the nightmare from which he'd emerged without his memories three years before.

"AWRIGHT, LADY." The cab driver stopped the car.

"But we're barely a hundred yards off the highway," Paige cried.

"I done tole you, lady, this all the far I go." He held his hand out, waiting for her to pay him. "You go more farther back in that crazy place, you got to walk yourself."

"And I told you, I'd give you more money if you would take me all the way."

He shook his head in wonder, as if he couldn't believe she didn't understand. "And I told you, this all the far I go."

Paige sighed and handed him the money. He was right. He had told her. And she didn't have any more money anyway.

As soon as she was clear of the car door he threw the car into reverse and hightailed it back to the highway.

Johnny had asked her to wait an hour before calling the police. She looked at the digital clock on the cell phone. It had been about thirty minutes. Was an hour long enough for Johnny to be sure Katie was safe? Was it too long? Was he in danger of being caught if she delayed?

"Damn it, Johnny, why didn't you wait for me?" she said out loud.

She looked in front of her. A long way ahead, the road disappeared into the brush. She studied the muddy shells beneath her feet. There had obviously been recent traffic. Were those tire tracks Johnny's?

She started walking, hoping she was doing the right thing.

TOTAL DARKNESS SURROUNDED him. Johnny pushed with his feet and hands, but he couldn't tell if he was moving or not. The water enveloped him like a shroud, encumbering him, imprisoning him, seeping into his clothes and burning his eyes and teasing his nostrils, coaxing him to breathe it in.

He kept swimming.

His hand brushed a slimy pole and he jerked away, disoriented. Confused, he turned all the way around in the water. Which way had he come from? Which way was he headed?

His lungs began to burn.

Then something darker than the dark appeared up ahead. Swallowing muddy water in his excitement, he pushed toward the darker form. As he grew closer, he saw that it was above him, so he kicked for the surface, not really allowing himself to hope that he would ever actually breathe again.

Just when he knew he couldn't hold his breath another instant, his hand exited the water and hit something solid.

He kicked again and his head emerged from the punishing black wetness.

He sucked in air, trying not to cough, his stomach heaving up the muddy water he'd swallowed. He retched and gagged, holding his hand over his mouth, muffling the sound. If he were caught now, then he and Katie would both be dead.

He wiped his face and pushed his wet hair back,

trying to orient himself to this pitch-black world he'd emerged into. There were only about two feet of clearance between the water and the wooden floor above him.

Floor? Was this the floor of the warehouse? He turned around in the water, looking everywhere, his heart fluttering in panic as he searched for a spot of light somewhere, anywhere.

Then he saw it. It was just a sliver, but it was light. He swam toward it, realizing how shaky his arms and legs were. Damn, what a coward he was, afraid of the dark.

The light turned out to be a square hole in the floor. Railroad ties were built up around the edges, but directly above his head were the steel rails and the boxcar. And there, in the center of the boxcar's base, was the trapdoor he remembered. The door he'd been deathly afraid was a fantasy. His limbs went weak with relief.

Now came the hard part. Could he get the door open and climb into the car without frightening his little girl to death?

He had to try.

He pushed on the door. Like the escape he'd designed from his father's house, like the window in his hotel room, he'd done everything he could to make this secret hideout easy to reach and fail-safe, so all during his teenaged years he'd kept the hinges of the door oiled and free from rust.

His care back then paid off now, because the door lifted without a sound. He pushed it open slowly, blinking away water from his eyes.

Then he saw her.

She was sitting on a cot holding a picture book,

dressed in blue jeans and a New Orleans Saints T-shirt, with only one sock. Little tennis shoes sat neatly on the floor near the cot.

She clutched an orange-and-green afghan around her and watched him with huge, dark-blue eyes.

"Hi, Katie," he said softly.

She lifted her little chin and looked around the brightly lit room, her gaze going to the sliding door then back to him. Her eyes went even wider and began to fill with tears.

Johnny longed to throw the trap door open and grab her, but he controlled himself with a great effort. He didn't want her to be more frightened of him than of the guard who brought her movies and books.

"Can I come in for a minute? I got all wet." He spoke softly and didn't move a muscle.

She backed up on the bed and pulled the afghan closer.

He smiled at her, praying he didn't look like a sea monster. "I'm a friend of your mom's."

A tiny frown line appeared between her eyes and she looked past him into the gap made by the trap door. "My mom?" she whispered. "Is my mommy coming?"

"No, but if you'll let me come in we can go find her."

"Are you a bad guy?"

Johnny shook his head solemnly. "No, Katie. I'm the good guy. I'm here to rescue you."

She looked at him for a moment. "The villains locked me in here."

"I know they did. Are you ready to be rescued?"

She watched him for a few seconds without blinking. He didn't even dare to breathe.

"Okay."

His head throbbing with relief, Johnny slowly climbed into the boxcar without taking his eyes off his daughter.

"Hi, Katie," he said. "My name is Johnny." He crouched down before the cot and held out his hand to her.

He couldn't stop looking at her. She was his child. His little girl. A living miracle, a testament to Paige's beauty and bravery and determination. Whatever it took, he had to put her back into her mother's loving, sheltering arms.

Katie didn't move to take his hand. She pulled the afghan tighter and stared at him. "You look scary," she said in a quivery little voice.

"I know." He nodded and spread his hands. "My clothes are all wet. But your mom sent me to get you. Aren't you ready to go see her?" he asked, his throat closing with emotion now that he was actually here, seeing his child for the first time. "Can I show you something your mom gave me?"

She didn't respond.

Slowly, he straightened, and dug carefully in the pocket of his jeans. With the utmost care, he extracted the soaked school picture Paige had given him and laid it on the cot beside Katie.

"See what your mom gave me? It was so you'd know I was her friend and you'd let me rescue you from the villains."

Katie looked at the picture without moving. "That's my mom's picture from her purse. It has the broken corner."

"That's right."

"Why didn't Mommy come to get me?" she asked, her voice filling with tears.

"She's calling the police to catch the bad guys. But I'm here to take you to her. Will you go with me?"

He held out his hands, not really expecting the child to trust him. She was certainly her mother's daughter. She had to consider every option carefully before she would commit.

So he was almost knocked over with surprise when she stood up and held out her arms. "Will you take me to my mommy?" she asked quietly.

"I will, Katie. I swear I will."

She leapt at him, wrapping her arms and legs around his wet body, clinging to him with all the unrestrained trust of a child. His eyes filled with tears as his daughter's arms tightened around his neck and her soft blond hair, so much like her mother's, tickled his cheek.

An overwhelming warmth and yearning spread through him, making his heart ache. She was his and he was hers. Connected.

He was no longer Jay Wellcome, nobody. He was a father; a lover; a son. He was John Andrew Yarbrough, and his daughter was depending on him. He hugged her for a brief, awesome moment before he spoke.

"Listen to me, Katie. We have to do something very scary to get out of here. Are you brave?"

She nodded against his neck. "My mom says I have courage."

"You do." He blinked and hugged her tightly. "Now if I were to tell you we were going swimming, would that be okay?"

"I had swimming lessons last year."

"How about holding your breath. Can you do that?"

She leaned back in his arms and looked at him. "That was the first lesson," she said indignantly.

"Good. That's really good, because we've got to go under the water and hold our breaths."

"I can do that."

"Now, Katie, listen to me."

She looked up at him with the same dark blue eyes he saw in the mirror every day.

"I'm real scared of the water," he whispered. "Can you hold on to me real tight so I won't be scared?"

She nodded silently.

"And you won't let go no matter what? You'll hold on to my neck and keep me safe until we can pull our heads above water?"

She nodded.

"Show me how you hold your breath."

Katie took a big breath and held it and squeezed his neck tightly.

Tears burned his eyes as her little arms tightened around him. "That's good, Katie. Are you ready to go?"

"Yes, sir."

Johnny wrapped his arms tightly around her and hugged her. "You have a lot of courage, Katie," he said. "Like your mom. A lot more than me. Now we're going to slide into the water real quiet, and then we'll take a big breath, and go under the water and back up before you can count to twenty-seven. Can you count to twenty-seven?"

She giggled nervously. "Yes."

"Count slow, and don't let go for anything." He

kissed her soft hair and cradled her head with his hand, then slipped through the trap door. Her little body stiffened as they sank into the water.

"Okay, you're doing great. Let's take three big breaths and we'll go on the third one."

"Okay," she said. "Don't worry, I won't let you go."

So with his daughter following his movements, Johnny took a deep breath and let it out, then a second, then a third, and nodded to his child.

Katie closed her eyes and tightened her hold on his neck.

Praying for as much strength as his daughter had, Johnny ducked them both into the water and dove downward, kicking furiously and pushing against the water with one arm, while the other held his precious cargo.

He swam as fast and as smoothly as he could, feeling Katie's little arms squeezing him, until he saw a faint glow. He headed for it. To his amazement, they were already out from under the building. He swam toward the light.

When their heads broke the surface, they were under the pier. He pushed wet hair out of his face and looked at his daughter, who was still holding on to him and still holding her breath, her eyes squeezed tightly closed.

"You can breathe now, Katie, but be quiet, okay?" he whispered.

She let go her stranglehold on his neck and pushed her wet hair away from her face. "That was only eighteen," she whispered.

Her words surprised him. "How slow were you counting?"

"One-Mississippi, two-Mississippi," she said, "like my mom taught me."

Johnny laughed softly and hugged her. "Only eighteen, wow," he said. "It felt like eight hundred to me."

She grinned at him and shook water out of her hair.

"Now I'm going to take you to where your mom is waiting for us."

He looked around quickly, but nothing had changed. The sun was not even noticeably lower in the sky. He suppressed a shudder. That meant getting into the railroad car and back out had taken no more than fifteen minutes total. It had seemed like hours. He pulled them both out of the water.

After retrieving his gun and putting his shoes on, he picked Katie up again.

"Where's my mommy?" she asked, her little voice trembling.

He kissed her soft little cheek. "We'll see your mommy real soon." He started pushing his way through the rice grass and reeds, dodging the Spanish moss that draped the cypress trees like gray shrouds, headed toward his home and the highway. Then he remembered Miss Aileen and Mr. Woodrow's house. He could get back to the warehouse in plenty of time to arrange a surprise for his stepmother if he didn't have to walk all the way through the swamp to the highway.

"You know what, Katie? There's a nice lady who used to live over here at the very end of the bayou. She fed me gumbo and let me play with her puppies. Maybe she still has some puppies."

"Puppies?" Katie repeated, her voice rising in interest.

"Yeah. And I'll bet she'll let you play with them until I go get your mom."

He turned west and walked along the edge of the bayou until he came to the old house where Miss Aileen and Mr. Woodrow lived.

He stepped up onto the porch and knocked on the door.

The door creaked as a small, gray-haired woman opened it a crack. "Who you want?" she said, then stopped, staring.

"Is that a zombie?" She flung the door wide, her mouth stretching into a gap-toothed grin. "'Cause it can't be young Johnny. Come in here, *chér*. We thought you was dead. Who's that little one and what are you doing soaking wet?"

Johnny grinned. "Not quite dead, Miss Aileen."

Chapter Thirteen

Paige stared in the window of the abandoned blue rental car, her heart pounding in her ears. It had been one of the hardest things she'd ever done, walking up to that car, afraid of what she'd find, but thank God it was empty.

She looked at the cell phone's clock. Forty minutes had passed since Johnny had left her. She didn't care if it hadn't been an hour yet. She was calling the police now.

She didn't know whether he had decided to go the rest of the way on foot, or if he somehow had been overpowered and forced to leave his car.

She prayed he was all right. As furious as she was at him for leaving her at the gas station, she loved him for putting himself in danger for the daughter he'd never known. She loved him for his courage; courage he hadn't possessed seven years ago.

It occurred to her that while she'd never stopped loving him, she'd never forgiven him either. Not even after she'd thought he was dead. He *should* have been brave enough to take her with him to confront his father and his stepmother.

How different their lives might have been if they'd

walked together down Urselines that long-ago afternoon. She wouldn't have spent all those months alone and scared, with no idea how she was going to care for a baby. She wouldn't have had to be both father and mother to Katie, wouldn't have had to raise her alone.

If Johnny had taken her with him that fateful day, Katie would have had her father. She'd have had the best schools, the most beautiful clothes. She would have been so happy.

Paige froze, horrified at her thoughts. What was she thinking? She wouldn't change one day of her life with her beautiful daughter. Not for anything.

She had learned how to survive, how to be strong, because of Katie. She'd learned how to live, instead of just existing.

She didn't regret anything.

Now Johnny was risking his life to save their child. She had to get help for him. With shaky fingers, she dialed 911 on the cell phone. When the dispatcher answered, she stammered at first, trying to figure out exactly how to explain what was happening.

"Is this an emergency?" the efficient voice said.

"Yes. My little girl has been kidnapped," she said, working to control her voice.

"Tell me your name please."

"Paige Reynolds. My daughter's name is Katie. Her father is John Andrew Yarbrough. He's gone to save her but we need the police."

"Where are you located, ma'am?"

Paige heard an engine behind her. She turned and looked. It was a large SUV. She ducked down behind the blue car.

"Bayou Lesgensfou," she said quickly. "The old

warehouse.'' The SUV was coming closer. ''Please hurry. They're here.''

''Ma'am, I need you to stay on the phone.''

''They're here. I'll leave the phone on, but please, send the police to the warehouse. Bayou Lesgensfou. My daughter's being held there.''

''Wait, ma'am—''

Paige threw the phone into the bushes as the SUV slowed to a stop. They'd seen the car, and in a minute they would see her.

She ran, knowing it wouldn't do any good. But maybe she could lead them away from the warehouse. Maybe she could delay them long enough for the police to come. Long enough for Johnny to get Katie to safety.

The SUV turned and came after her. Paige's heart pounded and her breath whooshed in her ears as she ran as fast as she could over the rough shell road and into the underbrush.

But she wasn't fast enough. The big utility vehicle easily overtook her and a man jumped out holding a shotgun.

''I wouldn't go no further if I was you,'' the man said in a nasal twang.

She stopped and held her hands up, breathing in great, wheezing gasps. She wanted to cry in frustration, but she would never let Serena Yarbrough see one single tear.

''Now why don't you and me take a walk? Sis can follow in the car.''

Paige wiped sweat off her face with the back of one hand as she glanced at the SUV. Was that Serena driving?

"Let's go." The man's voice was harsh. He was tired of waiting.

"Okay," she gasped, and turned. They walked toward the warehouse with Serena following in the SUV.

When Paige got her first glimpse of the battered wooden building, she almost cried out in horror and relief. Her throat closed up and her heart squeezed.

This was the warehouse Johnny had remembered. Katie was in there! So close. She suppressed a reckless urge to break into a run, screaming Katie's name.

Had Johnny had time to find her? Were they still inside?

"Why are you doing this?" she asked the man, stalling for time. "What is that building?"

"Don't be stupid." The man spit tobacco juice near her feet. She smelled the stale, bitter odor of tobacco on his breath. "You know your kid's in there. Ain't that why you came?"

She felt the barrel of the shotgun press into her back. She kept walking.

The SUV's engine stopped and a car door slammed. Paige turned. It was Serena. The white streak slashed through her black hair like an open wound. She pushed it back from her face with a scarlet-tipped nail as she picked her way carefully along the shell road, her high heels sinking into the dirt and crunching the shells.

"Hello, Paige," she said, smiling blandly.

Helpless, virulent anger surged through Paige. "You!" she grated, as the man prodded her again. For an instant, Paige considered attacking Serena with her bare hands, but the rational part of her brain knew she wouldn't make it two steps before the man shot her.

She stared at the woman who had tried to kill Johnny twice, and who was holding their daughter hostage.

''Where's my stepson?'' Serena walked up close to her.

Paige lifted her chin. ''Where's my daughter?''

''Leonard,'' Serena said.

The man came up and grabbed Paige's arm. ''My sister asked you a question.'' He twisted and pain radiated through her sore shoulder and all the way down to her wrist.

She could hardly breathe. ''I don't know—where he is,'' she rasped. ''He left me.''

''You're lying.''

The man jerked on her arm again and agony shrieked through her as she felt something tear. She couldn't suppress a cry.

''My daughter,'' she gasped as the edges of her vision turned black. She blinked, trying not to give in to the pain. ''I want to—see her, now!''

''You want to see your daughter?'' Serena asked. ''Leonard, let's take Paige to see her daughter. We'll all wait for Johnny together. Because no matter what you say, Paige, I know my stepson. He'll be here. In fact, aren't you playing the little decoy? My guess is, he's hoping you'll distract us while he tries to sneak up on us. But we'll be ready for him.''

She shook her head, as if in regret. ''He always was too soft, too sentimental. He'll feel honor bound to protect you and his child.''

Leonard pushed Paige ahead of him to the side

door of the warehouse. He knocked with the butt of the gun.

The door slid open, and a large man with a cigarette dangling from his lips stood there with a handgun.

"Get outside, Martin. Keep an eye out." Leonard pushed Paige into the brightly lit building. "We're expecting Johnny any time now. You got your cell phone? Call when you see him and make sure he don't see you. Then when he tries to get in we'll get the drop on him. It'll be a nice little welcome back party for him."

Serena stepped inside and Martin walked out, pushing the door closed.

Paige looked around frantically. There was an old railroad car in the center of the room, and a lot of piled-up wood and debris. The smell of rotten fish was overwhelming. Over to one side was a battered wooden crate. She stared at it in horrified fascination. *That was where they'd held Johnny.*

"Where is my child?" she shouted. "Katie!"

"You'll be with her very soon," Serena said. "Soon and for eternity. As soon as Johnny gets here. And by the way, throwing the phone away was a very stupid move. It almost got your little girl killed."

"What is the matter with you?" Paige cried, pain creating a haze through which it was hard to think. "You're a mother! How can you stand there and talk about killing my little girl when you have a child of your own?"

"Leave my son out of this. Now where is Johnny?"

"I told you I don't know."

Serena sighed. "I suppose I gave him too much

credit. I can't believe it took him this long to figure out that his daughter was being held in the same warehouse he'd been in.''

Paige recalled Johnny's description of his prison. The rough wood walls, the sounds, the darkness.

The darkness.

"Katie!!" she screamed, and broke away from Leonard to run toward the crate. "Katie! Answer me!''

"Hey!" Leonard overtook her and grabbed her arm again.

Pain stole Paige's senses for an instant and she stumbled, but she kicked out blindly, and was rewarded by a grunt of pain. "Let my daughter out of there!''

Serena laughed. "She's not in that nasty crate. I wouldn't do that to a child. Besides, I'm saving it for my stepson. Leonard, let poor Paige see her daughter. They can have a nice little reunion before Johnny gets here.''

Paige tried to break away from Leonard again, but this time he was ready. She couldn't break his hold.

He dragged her over to the car and turned the crank that unlocked the door. "You two can have a nice long visit, before the building accidentally burns down.''

Paige sent a disgusted glance at Serena. "You wouldn't put a child in that awful box, but you'd burn us alive?''

Serena sucked on her cigarette and waved away the smoke. "One has one's limits," she remarked.

Metal creaked as Leonard slid the boxcar door aside.

Paige held her breath, her heart pounding in her

throat, her arms aching for her child. Thank God! Her daughter was on the other side of that door.

"Hello, Serena."

It was Johnny!

He stood just inside the door of the boxcar, looking like a swamp creature, his gun leveled at Serena.

Paige felt all the blood drain from her head. Was she seeing things? Where was Katie? Her legs gave out from under her and her vision turned black. She fought to stay conscious as she collapsed to the floor.

Johnny stood on the balls of his feet, gun ready. He was aware of Paige's limp body sinking to the floor, but his attention was concentrated on the shotgun in the man's hand.

Before the man could recover from the shock of seeing him, Johnny jumped, kicking at the gun and knocking him to the floor, banging his head on one of the steel rails. He punted the shotgun halfway across the warehouse.

"Johnny! Look out!"

Paige's voice alerted him in time to whirl and grab Serena as she reached into her purse.

He flung the purse containing the little handgun toward Paige, sparing a glance at the dazed man, then leveled his gun at Serena.

"Hello, Stepmother," he said. "Been a while, hasn't it?"

"You bastard!" she screamed, curling her fingers into talons and scratching at his face. He stepped backward, out of her reach.

"How did you get in there?" she shrieked. "Where is that little brat of yours?"

Johnny's finger itched on the trigger. He took a long breath and suppressed the urge to take revenge for what this woman had done to him and his loved ones. "You probably should be careful, Serena. I'm a little upset about how you treated my daughter."

"You have no right to even speak to me. You always were a spoiled punk."

"Oh, I have a right to do a lot more than just talk," Johnny said, glancing sidelong at Paige, who was trying to crawl toward the railroad car.

"Paige," he called without turning his back on his stepmother. "Katie's not here. She's safe."

In his peripheral vision, he saw her go limp.

He heard sirens wailing in the distance, getting stronger. Paige had called the police. Good for her!

Serena heard them too, and her face blanched. "Listen, Johnny. I never meant to harm you. My brother forced me—"

"Save it, Stepmother," Johnny snapped as police kicked the door open and swarmed inside, yelling at him to put the gun down. He complied. "You married my father for his money and did everything you could to turn him against me. I remember how you goaded him, telling him he was too lenient on me, that if he encouraged my drawing, he was just encouraging the weakness you said I'd inherited from my mother. You wanted him to despise me, but it didn't work. In fact, he ended up despising you, didn't he? He would have divorced you if it hadn't been for my brother."

"You don't know what you're talking about." Serena jerked her arm away from the policeman who tried to restrain her.

"You'd be surprised what I know. And you can be sure I'll be asking the police to take another, closer look into my father's death."

When an officer approached him, Johnny held up his hands, knowing he'd have some explaining to do.

With a bansheelike scream, Serena lunged at him again, and the officer grabbed her. "Your father hated you," she shrieked.

He smiled and shook his head, the words from his father's letter echoing in his heart. "No. You're wrong. It was you who hated me. My father loved me."

SOMEONE WAS HOVERING OVER Paige, calling her name. It was a familiar, beloved voice. She opened her eyes and looked into dark-blue ones.

"Johnny?" she croaked.

"Hey, Tiger." He smiled and touched her face. "How are you feeling?"

"What happened? Where's Katie?" Paige was on some kind of cot. She moved to sit up, but her head was still fuzzy and something was holding her down.

"You're in an ambulance. You fainted."

She blinked. "I did not."

Then memories flooded her and fear choked her throat. "Where's Katie? Where's my baby?"

Johnny moved backward a bit. "She's right here. Come on, Katie. It's okay."

"Mommy!"

That precious voice, that beautiful little face. Paige reached for her daughter, but screaming pain in her shoulder stopped her. She cried out.

"Sir, we need to be careful. Her shoulder is almost certainly broken."

Paige strained to turn her head. An emergency medical technician sat at the head of the cot, out of her line of sight.

Johnny nodded. "Be gentle, Katie. Remember what I told you? Your mommy's shoulder is hurt. We have to be careful with her until the doctors can fix it."

"Can I hug her?"

Paige laughed and cried at the same time. "Oh, sweetheart, you can hug me as hard as you want. Come here and give me a big hug and kiss."

Her little girl's arms went around her neck and she planted big, wet kisses all over her face and neck. Paige put her right arm around her little girl and hugged her back, ignoring the pain. She sobbed with relief to have her child back with her again, safe and whole and beautiful.

After a moment, she opened her eyes and looked over Katie's head at Johnny.

He was watching the two of them with an odd look on his face, a look almost of sadness.

"What happened?" she whispered, kissing her daughter's hair. "How did you do that? Get inside that railroad car?"

Katie kissed Paige full on the mouth and then sat up. "Mommy, this is Johnny. He saved me. I helped him be brave."

Paige stared at them both. "You did?"

"Uh-huh. He came up in the floor and we had to go under the water to get away from the villains. He was scared, but I had courage."

Paige had no idea what her daughter was talking about, but she did know Katie had courage. She kissed her again. "I know you did. You are so brave. Are you okay?"

"Katie's going to be checked at the hospital too," Johnny said. "Just to be sure." He tugged gently on

Katie's hair. "You want to come sit on my lap and let your mom rest?"

Katie clung to her mother for a few more seconds, then to Paige's amazement, she let Johnny pick her up and set her on his knee.

"Johnny?" Paige said, trying to move into a position that wouldn't hurt. She moaned.

The EMT put his hand on her right shoulder. "Try to move as little as possible, ma'am. I've given you something for pain, and you'll be more comfortable real soon."

Johnny wrapped his arm around his daughter and kissed the top of her head. Paige's heart turned upside down to see the tenderness with which he treated the child he'd only just met.

"What happened to Serena?" she asked.

"You surprised Serena's brother when you collapsed, and I was able to kick the shotgun out of his hand." He raised a brow. "Do you remember warning me to watch out for Serena?"

She shook her head.

"Well, you did. She was reaching into her purse for her gun, and I was able to get it away from her. Right about then the police arrived." He shrugged. "That was pretty much it."

Paige doubted that was it, but before she could ask any more questions, the ambulance turned into the hospital emergency entrance and there was a flurry of activity while she was transported into the emergency room.

After they'd cut her clothes off and started an IV and given her a sedative, they let Johnny and Katie see her again.

When Johnny walked in with Katie in his arms,

Paige realized he was wet and dirty, his bandage was filthy and unraveling, and his hair was tousled and damp. Her entire being was flooded with love for him.

He had done what he'd promised. He'd brought her child safely back to her. She realized her daughter's life, and her own would never be the same again.

Her daughter had her father. It was obvious Johnny loved his child, and Katie adored him.

The nurse spoke. "You only have a few minutes. Ms. Reynolds is on her way to surgery, to have that shoulder set." She smiled. "She's been sedated."

Johnny held Katie over Paige so she could kiss her. Katie giggled at being held suspended in the air. Paige kissed her daughter on the nose and on the mouth, then Johnny swung his little girl back up into his arms.

Paige laughed sleepily at Katie, who was nearly swallowed by a blue scrub shirt. "Where did you get those clothes, Katie?"

"The nurse let me have it. Mine were all wet."

Paige blinked. It was getting harder to hold her eyes open. "The nurse wouldn't let you have new clothes?" she asked Johnny.

He shook his head, a small smile on his face. "I said I'd wait until you two were taken care of."

"Johnny, I can't—"

"Paige, I'm sorry—"

They both spoke at once, then stopped.

Katie looked at her mother and then at Johnny. She put her hand on the side of his face and made him look at her. "Are you my daddy?" she asked.

Paige's heart stopped for an instant. She held her breath. What would he say to his child?

He swallowed, and in the bright emergency room

lights, Paige saw wetness glittering in his eyes. He blinked.

"How would you feel about that?" he asked, his voice raspy with emotion.

Paige bit her lip and waited.

Katie looked at him solemnly. "I think you have to be my daddy, because you came under the water to get me even though you were scared."

Paige suppressed a sob and tears leaked out of her eyes.

Katie looked at her. "Mommy, if he's my daddy, he should come live with us, right?"

"Katie…" She looked helplessly at Johnny, her mind hazy with the drugs they'd given her. She couldn't find the right words.

Johnny sent her a sharp look, then smiled sadly at Katie and touched her cheek.

Paige couldn't interpret the expression on his face. Apprehension took hold of her throat, squeezing the breath out of her.

"Katie," he said. "Sometimes mommies and daddies don't live together. But I will always be your daddy."

Paige's very soul ached. She moaned involuntarily.

Johnny put Katie down and leaned over the gurney to whisper in Paige's ear. "We need to talk. But not here. Not now. You're about to go to sleep on me."

As if on cue, the nurse threw back the curtain. "They're ready for you, Ms. Reynolds."

Johnny pressed a kiss to her forehead as an orderly came in and unlocked the gurney.

"Katie," she cried.

Johnny picked up Katie again so she could see her mom.

"Say goodbye quickly," the nurse said. "Mommy's got to get her shoulder fixed. You stay here with Daddy."

Paige smiled sleepily at her daughter. "Stay with Daddy, Katie. He'll take care of you." Johnny held Katie so she could kiss her mom one more time.

"Bye, Mommy," he said with a smile.

Paige struggled to speak through the growing haze of the drugs. "You'll be here when I get out of surgery, won't you?"

Johnny glanced down at the top of Katie's head then back at her, his gaze guarded. "I have some things I have to take care of. But I'll be back as soon as I can."

Paige tried to read the expression on his face, but she couldn't. Why was he avoiding her gaze?

The last thing she saw as the orderly wheeled her out of the room was her daughter putting her arms around her father's neck and kissing his cheek.

SERENA'S LUXURY TOWN HOME in Diamondhead was impressive, from the high stone walls that surrounded the community to the manned security gate. As Johnny walked up the steps to ring the doorbell, he took in the manicured lawn, the Mexican-tiled walkway and entry, the beveled glass and mahogany door. He considered the amount of wealth represented in the exclusive community.

He had once been a part of this kind of life. Even though his memory was almost fully returned, it seemed so foreign to him now. Foreign in more ways than material.

The door opened and a uniformed housekeeper

looked at the identification papers he carried. "Child Services has talked to you, right?"

She nodded and stood back to let him in.

"Where is Brandon?" he asked her.

"He's in the media room, watching television. Right through here."

He followed her through the richly appointed hall to the media room that was large and plush, the indirect lighting and strategically placed and expensively designed speakers adding to the luxurious, hushed atmosphere.

A little boy with black hair was watching cartoons on a giant TV screen recessed into the wall.

"Brandon?" The child turned around. His blue eyes were striking under the shock of black hair.

"Hi, Brandon, I'm Johnny."

"Hi," Brandon said shyly.

Johnny went over and knelt down in front of the leather couch where his little half brother sat.

"Do you know who I am?"

Brandon nodded. "The lady told me."

"Did she tell you we're brothers?"

The boy studied Johnny. He waited without moving, until Brandon could get used to his presence.

"You're old for a brother."

Johnny smiled. "I know. But I have a little girl who's not very much older than you. Would you like to go meet her?"

"When will I get to see my mama?" Brandon asked.

Johnny sighed. Hadn't the social worker told the child about Serena?

"You'll get to see her soon. Right now why don't

you come with me? Katie is staying with some nice
people who have puppies.''

"Puppies?" The child's eyes lit up.

"Yeah. Want to go see them?"

Brandon jumped off the couch and ran to the door.
"Mrs. Carter, can I go with Mr. Johnny to see some
puppies?"

The housekeeper came down the staircase with a
small suitcase. Her eyes were glistening. "Sure you
can. You be a good boy, okay?"

She handed the suitcase to Johnny. "Please take
care of him. He loves his mother very much."

"Thank you, Mrs. Carter. He'll be fine." Johnny
leaned down and picked up Brandon, then took the
suitcase in his other hand as Mrs. Carter opened the
door for him.

"I like you for a brother. You're big and strong."

Johnny smiled and kissed the top of the five-year-
old's head. "I like you for a brother too," he said,
his voice cracking.

JOHNNY SHIFTED THE bouquet of flowers from one
hand to the other as he waited for the elevator to stop
on Paige's floor. He'd taken Katie and Brandon to
stay with Miss Aileen while he dealt with the police.

He'd spent the last twelve hours going over the
events of the past days, as well as the events of three
years before with police detectives, crime scene in-
vestigation teams, and lawyers. He'd identified the
two men who'd chased them and tried to kill them.
He'd spent hours answering questions about his kidnapping and about his stepmother. And he'd been fin-
gerprinted and grilled to prove his identity.

Now he finally had a few minutes to see Paige.

The last time he'd checked on her she'd still been sedated from her surgery.

It was late, and the lights were dim on the orthopedic ward. He stopped in front of her closed door, took a deep breath, and pushed his fingers through his hair.

He had no idea what he was going to say to her, other than *I'm sorry*.

He had so much to be forgiven. He just hoped she could find it in her heart to give him another chance.

He knocked lightly on the door, then pushed it open. The room was dim, only the recessed light above the bed was on.

Paige lay with her eyes closed, her face almost as pale as the white pillows behind her head. Her left arm was bandaged, and faint purple smudges were evident under her eyes.

She'd been through so much.

He looked around and didn't see any place to put the flowers, so he laid them on the foot of the bed, then sat down beside her.

After a few minutes, she opened her eyes.

"Hi, Tiger," he said softly, carefully touching her right hand, where an IV catheter protruded from her delicate, bandaged wrist.

"You came back," she whispered, her eyes drifting shut. "After all this time."

"Paige?" She still seemed heavily sedated. Was she dreaming?

She opened her eyes again. "Where's Katie? Is she okay?" She licked her lips.

"The doctors pronounced her perfectly healthy, even after the dousing in the bayou. She and Brandon are with Miss Aileen. They're fine. They're playing with a new litter of puppies.''

"Brandon? Oh, Serena's son. Your stepbrother.''

"I talked to Children's Services and as his brother, I've got temporary custody. I couldn't see leaving him in Serena's ultramodern condo with nobody there but the housekeeper.''

She frowned and forced her eyes to focus on his face. "They've given me too much medication.''

"You need to just lie there and enjoy it. You've been through a lot.''

"What happened with Serena?'' Paige asked, trying to sit up a little straighter in the bed. "They got her, didn't they?''

Johnny nodded. "She's locked up, as is her brother, but she'll probably be out on bail soon. Her lawyer is trying to go for a plea of diminished capacity, but it's beginning to look like her weasel of a brother may sell her out for a reduced sentence. Personally, I think she is insane. Leonard is hinting that she murdered my dad.''

"Oh, Johnny, I'm sorry.''

He nodded. "Me too.''

"What about you? Is your arm okay? You didn't give me a chance to bandage it. You left me.'' Paige's voice thickened and tears shone in her eyes.

Johnny felt like a heel. "I didn't want to put you in danger.''

"I was so mad at you, and so scared.''

"I know.'' He reached up and caught a tear from her lashes on his fingertip. "I couldn't risk your life too. I should have known better than to think you'd stay put.''

She closed her eyes, savoring the brief, featherlike touch of his finger against her skin.

"Paige," he said, a new tone in his voice. "I need you to understand something."

A shard of fear lodged in her breast. "What is it?" she asked softly, steeling herself. No matter what he said, she could handle it. She wasn't like her mother, living in limbo, waiting for a man who would never return.

She'd lived through losing him before. It wouldn't be easy, but she could live through it again.

The important thing was that her daughter had her father.

Johnny's hand caught a strand of her hair and entwined it in his fingers. His gaze roamed over her face, her eyes, her mouth.

"I remember your spiky hair," he whispered. "I remember making love with you for hours and hours, until we both were too tired to move."

Paige's heart twisted inside out. She remembered too. All of it. She'd never forgotten one moment of their time together and she never would.

He pushed the strand of hair behind her ear, then traced her jaw line with his finger. "I didn't have the courage to go to my father with you by my side and say, *Here, this is the girl I want to marry.* He'd listened too long to Serena's lies. And so had I."

Her breath caught in her throat.

"So like a coward, I left you there alone. I was coming back the next day, but—" He stopped, and her heart stopped at the same time.

She blinked and another tear fell down her cheek. "We were young, Johnny. I know that. Too young. You had your whole career ahead of you."

He put his fingers over her lips. "Could you just let me talk for a minute?"

He brushed the wetness off her cheek. "It took me a long time, but the memory of what happened that day finally came back to me. There was an accident. My car was totaled. When I woke up in the hospital they'd put a pin in my hip."

"The scar," she whispered.

"I tried to find you, but by the time I got out of the hospital, you had disappeared. Your landlord had no idea where you'd gone. I went down to the French Quarter every chance I got. I hired a private detective, but I didn't tell him to look anywhere but around New Orleans. I should have searched every city in every state."

His eyes reflected old sadness and pain. "I am so sorry. I should have never left you there that day."

Paige heard his words, but it took her hazy brain a while to process them. He'd been in an accident. He hadn't walked out deliberately. Not like her father had.

"After my mother died, I found my father's name among her things," she said, looking down at a frayed string on the blanket. "He was a locally famous trial lawyer. Carlson Page. She named me after him."

She shook her head and smiled sadly. "I went to his office and asked to see him. I just wanted to meet him and tell him my mother had died. I told his secretary I was Maxine Reynolds's daughter. When the secretary came back, she said Mr. Page was busy, but could one of the junior partners help me."

She shrugged and looked up. "He didn't want to see me."

Johnny's face was shadowed, his eyes haunted. "I'm not like your father—"

She stopped him with a look. "I went to the Yarbrough Building once, too. I asked for you, but the security guard wanted to know if you were expecting me." She gave a sad little laugh. "I had to say no."

"Oh God, Paige. I know I can never make up for not trying hard enough to find you, but—"

"Johnny, don't. You're right. You're not my father. When you found out you had a daughter, you never hesitated. Not for an instant. You saved her." She touched his hand. "You are no coward. You're the bravest person I've ever known. You faced your darkest fear and conquered it to save our child."

He shook his head. "You're wrong on two counts. You are the brave one. And I'm facing my darkest fear right now, because I'm deathly afraid you're going to say no."

"Say no? To what?"

"Can you trust me enough to believe I will never walk away from you again? Can you trust me enough to marry me, Paige Reynolds?"

Paige's heart fluttered like a hummingbird in her breast. "M-marry you?" she repeated.

An amused look lit his face. "M-m-marry me," he said. "Be my wife. Help me make my little brother feel safe and loved. Make a home for you and Katie and Brandon and me. Love me forever."

Paige felt the tears slipping from her eyes and flowing down her face. "Oh, Johnny."

"Hey, why the tears? I love you."

Paige heard the words she thought had died long ago, along with her dream. "Say that again," she demanded.

Johnny leaned over and kissed her gently but thoroughly. "I love you, I love you, I love you," he said against her lips.

"I love you too, John Andrew Yarbrough. Now call the nurse and get me out of here, because I'm not ever letting you out of my sight again."

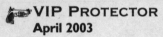
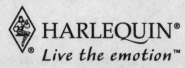

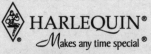

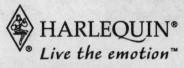